For Richer, For Richest

Switched at Marriage, Episode 5

Gina Robinson

Gina Robinson
SEATTLE, WASHINGTON

www.ginarobinson.com

Publisher's Note: This is a work of fiction. Names, characters, places, and incidents are a product of the author's imagination. Locales and public names are sometimes used for atmospheric purposes. Any resemblance to actual people, living or dead, or to businesses, companies, events, institutions, or locales is completely coincidental.

Book Layout ©2013 BookDesignTemplates.com
Cover Photos and Design by Jeff Robinson

For Richer, For Richest, Switched at Marriage 5/ Gina Robinson. — 1st ed.
ISBN 978-0692492611

Also by
GINA ROBINSON

SWITCHED AT MARRIAGE ROMANCE SERIAL

Part 1, A WEDDING TO REMEMBER
Part 2, THE VIRGIN BILLIONAIRE
Part 3, TO HAVE AND TO HOLD
Part 4, FROM THIS DAY FORWARD
Part 5, FOR RICHER, FOR RICHEST

NEW ADULT ROMANCE

RUSHED
CRUSHED
HUSHED
RECKLESS LONGING
RECKLESS SECRETS
RECKLESS TOGETHER

THE AGENT EX SERIES

"Full of laughter, intrigue, and, of course, steamy spies." —*RT Book Reviews*

LICENSE TO LOVE
THE SPY WHO LEFT ME
DIAMONDS ARE TRULY FOREVER
LIVE AND LET LOVE
LOVE ANOTHER DAY

WOMEN'S FICTION

PINK SLIPPER

CHAPTER ONE

Kayla

Right. When locking gazes with my ex across a crowded room, it was almost impossible *not* to blink. Out of sheer shock that out of all the gin joints in this world, he'd showed up in the middle of mine. My new life and ideal moment. When the eyes of too many suspicious people were on me. That if I faltered, everyone would see. That Eric's timing was still so impeccably *bad* and ironically perfect. That fate had such a wry sense of humor as to toss him into the bar just as Justin was singing to me in his sexy voice, begging me not to forget him. Saying he thought we would work out in the end. That we didn't have to hurt each other. Did Jus really believe that? Or was it just part of the show we were always putting on?

Eric *would* choose the very moment when the lyrics wondered whether I would walk on by the ex, him. Or acknowledge him and call his name? And if I hadn't been on stage, I honestly didn't know what I would have done. Because seeing him, damn seeing him, squeezed my heart. And, like so many times before, all the good times came rushing back, obliterating the bad ones.

I was stunned that one old song from a movie decades old could embody the two situations I was in so perfectly. Damn you, eighties night!

For an instant, Eric looked as surprised as I was. I willed him to turn around and walk away. Go to another bar with his buddies.

His eyes narrowed. He set his classic, square jaw. I recognized the look on his face. I'd just unwittingly issued a challenge. Eric *never* backed down from a contest.

He grinned. That cocky former frat boy grin that made my heart race simply out of habit. Like Pavlov's dog. Yes, Eric had dumped me. Treated me badly. But there was still a reason I'd fallen for him in the first place. He oozed charm. When he wanted to. And sex appeal. He was athletic. Broad-shouldered. Confident in a sweetly swaggering way. He turned heads. Even now the crowd of Flashionistas was looking and whispering. And maybe wondering who the interloper was and how to meet him.

Eric was eating up the attention and stir he was causing. He got an evil glint in his eyes.

I tried to clear the shock off my face. But not soon enough. Sarah, who'd also known Eric in college, and our history, saw the look on my face and followed it to the source. She swiveled in her seat and froze as Eric whispered to his buddies. One of them peeled off, skirted the crowd, and headed to the karaoke DJ.

Eric and his cohorts walked directly through the crowd, parting it like the Red Sea, only without any Biblical good intentions.

Jus kept singing, apparently unperturbed. When I glanced at him, his eyes had the same glint and taste for battle as Eric's. Like he wasn't about to let Eric ruin our moment.

The Flashionista crowd buzzed with speculation. I froze, literally unable to move, as Eric jumped on stage, followed by his two buds. The thing about Eric—he had stage presence. Always had.

It was at that moment, too, that I noticed one of the female reporters who'd been hounding Jus and me, skulking in corner booth.

Damn, damn, damn it all to hell! Pardon my French, as Grandma would say.

I heard a tiny bit of swooning from the crowd, restrained, as if out of respect for Jus and the other bosses on stage. I swore beneath my breath as the a cappella moment was broken and strains of music blared, startling everybody. Like music in a karaoke bar was to be totally unexpected.

Eric and his gang grabbed mics. Lyrics popped up on the screen in front of us and behind us so the crowd could sing along.

Before I could protest, Eric grabbed my hand and went down on one knee, looking up at me mournfully. Like he was heartbroken and vulnerable as he broke into the chorus from "Don't You Want Me."

Nooooo! No, no, no. I did not. Want him. Or did I? I was too surprised to even think to pull my hand away.

The crowd's attention was riveted on us. The reporter was tapping away on her phone and snapping a picture.

Was my mouth hanging open? That was going to look lovely on the morning news.

For a flash of an instant, Riggins and Wylie didn't seem to know what hit them or how to react. Justin got a look like murder on his face. Then, without speaking a word to each other, Wylie broke off and headed toward the DJ.

Justin pulled my hand away from Eric's. Which took a bit of doing. Eric was holding on with a killer grip. He only "reluctantly" let go. It was all for show. It had to be.

Even bearded, Jus looked young compared to Eric, who was bulked up and clean shaved. I remembered the feel of Eric's cheeks right after he shaved—smooth as a baby's butt, as they say. I used to love rubbing my cheek against his.

Jus, however, had the superior voice. And an intensity about him that was hard to resist as he looked into my eyes and sang "Baby, I Love Your Way." Which you would think would have been a little high for him, but worked.

The Flash crowd of Justin's loyal staffers had been holding their collective breath. As Jus sang, they applauded. "Give it to him, boss!" "You've got him on the run, Justin!"

It might have been sucking up to the boss guy, but it seemed pretty genuine to me. Scanning the crowd, many were still wondering where Eric had come from and how he had the guts to try to take the stage from Jus.

Eric and company were undeterred. Eric grabbed my free hand and spun me away from Jus, singing an old REO Speedwagon tune, "Keep On Loving You." His voice was higher than Justin's and suited him well enough.

But the lyrics? Right. If he'd wanted to keep on loving me, he wouldn't have left. No one forced him. He'd walked out on me. And moved in with her. But he was just vain enough to be pissed that I'd "fallen" for someone else. And competitive enough to show even a billionaire that Eric's former girl was never getting over him. Because, you know, I had a history of *not* moving past Eric and our calamitous relationship. Eric breathed on me. His breath smelled disastrously like booze.

A string of curses raced through my mind. Of course, he'd already been drinking. That was what had given him the guts and bravado to stage a takeover of Justin's party. When Eric was drunk, he lost all inhibition and became competitive nearly to the point of murder.

He was just arrogant and belligerent, and dumb enough to try to put the little geek guy in his place. Eric, in his boozed-up confidence, couldn't stand a former "little boy" taking even his castoff girlfriend. I could see it in his face. And remembered how he used to make fun of Jus in college. And tease me about Jus having a crush on me.

Oh, yeah, this was highly personal. A matter of pride. Even though Eric didn't want me, losing me to someone like Jus made me less of a prize in the first place. And somehow diminished the prestige of dating me in college. Eric was a prick.

I wondered what his current girlfriend would think if she saw him on stage serenading me? Probably, she would think it was a big joke. And egg him on. And then give me a smug look because Eric was going home with her. Well, what did I care?

And then I realized, *What* did *I care?*

Except that Eric was making a spectacle of things. And now Jus had that determined look in his eyes. The look of a guy who'd been bullied before and refused to be again. So calculating it was almost chilling. No guy was going to get the best of him and make a fool of him in front of his peeps. I had to get Eric off the stage.

Jus grinned and nodded to Riggins, who gave him a thumbs-up as they broke into a Hall and Oates imitation, singing, "Kiss on My List" to me. Both posturing and playing up to me as if I were the prize and my kiss was the best thing around.

I had to do something. I puckered my lips and blew Riggins a kiss. He caught it on his cheek with an exaggerated motion. I kissed Jus on the cheek, leaving a big lipstick print half above, half in his beard. I turned to the crowd and shrugged modestly as two billionaires serenaded me. Pretending to weigh my options in my hands. Which one? Which one?

The crowd, in general, wouldn't know the history between Eric and me. You could see the confusion on their faces. What did this intruder think he was doing up there? Who was this guy? He had balls. Either that or Jus staged it to show how he'd swept me off my feet.

Eric laughed, too loudly. Drunken loudly. He was enjoying himself in the way that guys who liked to fight did. And if I wasn't careful, he might actually throw a punch. He'd been known to in college. He liked the adrenaline rush. And he was good with his fists. The other guy never came out looking pretty. Now that Jus was a more even match in size to Eric, he was fair game.

Eric nodded to his goon.

I held my breath.

Eric's friend bent the DJ's ear again. I relaxed. No brawl for the moment.

Jus had the blackest look I'd ever seen on him on his face. He was determined to play knight in shining armor and defend my honor, and his. I pleaded with him with my eyes to back off and let me deal with Eric. I even shook my head ever so slightly. I was sure I could find a way to ease Eric off the stage and out of the limelight.

Jus ignored me.

Eric took my chin in his hand and tipped my face to him, singing, "With or Without You" by U2. He didn't have Bono's vocal range, and it showed as he missed the high notes.

Eric was a decent singer. He'd dabbled in a frat band in college, playing guitar and singing lead. His voice was pleasant, but not powerful.

Justin's voice was deep and resonant. Much stronger than Eric's. He swooped in, took my face in his hands and stared into my eyes as he sang "Take My Breath Away" with Riggins singing backup.

Jus had arresting eyes and a penetrating way of looking at you that made you feel he saw only you. It could be intimidating when he wanted it to be. But it could also be sexy and intimate, as it was now. He was absolutely determined to upstage Eric. He looked so genuine that I almost believed him.

Eric slid his arms around my waist from behind and snuggled up to me as he broke into a chorus of "Don't Dream It's Over" with his guys singing backup.

Jus didn't break his grip on my face as he sang "Still Loving You."

We were an uneasy threesome on stage. At least my third of it was horribly ill at ease, sandwiched between my former lover and my pretend husband. Cross this fantasy off my list. Oh, wait! This was no fantasy. This was more like a nightmare.

Eric pulled me away from Justin and sang "Easy Lover" as he danced with me in a kind of eighties dirty dancing. Generally I loved dancing. But this was over the edge, as Eric tried to grind against me.

Justin looked like he could kill.

I shot Sarah a panicked look. When Jus cut in, and Jus was not a smooth dancer like Eric, I had to do something. She got out of her seat.

Eric sang "Maneater" to Jus. Hey, I wasn't the villain here.

Jus ignored him and sang to me—"Never Gonna Give You Up." His deep voice was perfect for the song. He sounded as good as the original, not karaoke-like at all. And I wondered, almost hoped for an insane instant, that he meant what he was singing. That he never would give me up.

Sarah had reached the DJ. I realized her intention. No, no. I couldn't...

She said something to the DJ, turned, nodded to me, and gave me a thumbs-up. Crap! I knew what she'd done. But sing a solo? I couldn't do it. I barely even sang in the shower when no one could hear me. I never sang in public. That was like having a nightmare where you're naked in class or on the bus or at work.

My mouth went dry. My pulse pounded in my ears just as the music changed to the song that was meant for me to sing. The lyrics popped up on screen. I knew this one. Mom had always been a Madonna fan.

I pulled completely away from Eric and wrapped my arms around Justin's neck, clearly showing I'd chosen him, hoping I could pull this off as I stared into his eyes. I had to choose Jus. I had no other choice. He was my husband. I was startled to realize that I *wanted* to choose him.

My mouth was so dry I could barely form words. My voice trembled as I started singing "Crazy for You" slightly off key.

I was butchering the song in a bad, embarrassing, karaoke way. And I wasn't even drunk. Which was the only way I'd usually even think of singing, even have the courage to. But I kept singing, smiling at Jus. Ignoring Eric.

Justin's face lit up. His eyes sparkled. I hadn't seen such a radiant expression since the first time we made love. He was obviously grateful. And pleased. I pitied him. Because my singing really was that earsplittingly awful. Any other time I would have been booed off stage.

But then a beautiful thing happened. Sarah came onstage, stood beside me, grabbed a mic from one of Eric's boys, and started singing with me. And Sarah had a beautiful voice. One by one, more and more female Flashionistas joined us. Some came onstage. Some sang in their seats. We were all singing to Jus.

Eric and his guys had to back down. When the song ended, the bar erupted in applause. I kissed Jus. Or Jus kissed me. I wasn't sure who started it. It seemed natural to kiss.

To my surprise, and relief, Eric backed off. He nodded to Jus and bowed to him, indicating Jus had won with a sweep of his arm. "You win this round, man."

The DJ got in the act, officially calling the match by playing "Another One Bites the Dust" as the Flashionistas sang along.

Jus, always a good sport, shook Eric's hand, but his eyes were steely. "This is an old college acquaintance of mine, a friend of Kayla's," Jus said for his staff's benefit. As if that explained everything. "He always did like to give me a bad time."

That was an understatement.

He slapped Eric on the back. "Good to see you again, Eric. Welcome to the party." He looked around for a waitress. "Somebody get these men a drink, on me." He nodded to Eric, dismissing him, and pulled me by the hand off the stage.

I was shaken. And impressed by the way Jus handled the situation. He didn't leave my side for the rest of the evening. He barely let go of my hand.

Eric and company had their drinks, hit on a few girls, and left.

I ran into Sarah in the bathroom. "Thanks for saving me out there."

She was leaning into the mirror, reapplying her lipstick. "Sorry to make you sing. I know how shy you are about it. But your voice isn't half bad."

"Damned by faint praise." I laughed. "Seriously. Thanks."

She nodded. "It was the only thing I could think of in the heat of the moment." She paused. "Eric hasn't changed. He's still hotter than he deserves to be."

I shrugged and leaned into the mirror, pretending to check my makeup in an effort to deflect further questions.

"Just how long ago did you and Eric break up?" She stared at me in the mirror.

I froze. I'd been dreading that question. But there was no use lying about facts that could easily be checked and couldn't be disputed. "A few weeks."

Her eyes went wide. "A few weeks? But you and Justin—"

I nodded. "I know. It was quick." I had to sell it. "But when it's right, you just know it." I took a deep breath. "You heard him sing to me tonight." I smiled at her. "Who could resist that voice?"

"Or the way he looks at you." She blotted her lipstick and turned around to lean against the counter and study me. "You're lucky to have a guy as totally adorable and sweet as Jus who loves you as much as he obviously does."

Or was simply a great actor. And, as I was learning, a master at manipulating even difficult personalities. Was he fooling everyone? Or was I the only one who saw through him?

He made love to me as often as I let him. But he hadn't once said, or even hinted, that he loved me. That he was falling in love with me. Or even that he thought he ever could. He was my good-time, bedtime guy. And I was his sexual playmate. But were we anything more than that to each other?

After I returned from the bathroom, Jus grabbed my hand and took me around, making our excuses and saying goodbye. We left the party earlier than anyone else and much earlier than I wanted to.

I called him on it when we were out on the sidewalk, walking hand in hand to our car. We always held hands in public. It was part of the show.

"You really are a party-pooping old man in a young guy's body! It's not even dark yet. Don't tell me you have to get home to work!" I couldn't help sounding exasperated.

He arched one eyebrow, looking dryly amused and shocked at my naivety. "And here I thought you were the one with the social IQ. We *had* to leave so the rest of the staff could relax and actually have fun." He paused and hit the button at the corner for the walk light. "They can't let their hair down with the big boss in their midst."

"Riggins is still there." Hah! I'd skewed Jus with his prized logic.

"If you look behind us, you'll see him on his way to his car, too."

I glanced over my shoulder. Sure enough, there was Riggins. He gave me a friendly wave and peeled off down another street.

Jus gave me an "I told you so" look and grinned roguishly to soften it. "It's an unwritten rule. Riggins and I show up. Buy everyone a drink or two. Sing a few karaoke songs. Mingle a few more minutes and leave. One at a time so it's not obvious we know we're no longer wanted."

"No!" I frowned at him.

He sighed dramatically and comically. "It's lonely at the top isn't just a saying."

"But they *love* you!"

"They love to see me joke around and make a fool out of myself singing karaoke with Riggins and Wylie." His voice became suddenly hard. "They got an *extra* show tonight. But we showed that douchebag."

I was taken aback at his anger over Eric crashing our party. "I was as surprised as you were. I had no idea Eric would show up. It was just dumb bad luck." I frowned back at Jus.

Jus let it drop. We didn't speak about it again until we got home.

In the penthouse, Jus set his keys on the counter, scooped Data up to cuddle, and turned to face me. "You were quiet in the car. Are you okay? I'm sorry if I upset you. I shouldn't have called Eric a douche, even if he is. He treated you like shit when you were together, Kay. Even you can't deny it."

He stroked Data's chin and cooed to the puppy. "But you saw something in him, so there must be *some* good in him." He didn't sound convinced.

"Running into him so soon after breaking up is pretty shitty." He smiled at the dog. "And what was up with that act about wanting you back? I thought he was with someone else? And you're married."

"He was drunk and showing off. He *doesn't* want me. But he's used to me pining away for him, ready to take him back at a moment's notice after he's done straying. Now he's furious you've taken me, and that option, away. It's like not wanting anyone else to have a toy you don't want anymore. Pure selfishness and vanity." I had been holding it together pretty well, I thought. Until I glanced at Data in Justin's arms and realized I was jealous of a puppy. *I* wanted Justin's arms around me.

Jus saw the look on my face and held one arm out at me. "Come here. Family hug!"

I threw myself into him and let him cradle me with one arm. Data barked and squirmed to be let down. He set her on the floor and pulled me into a full hug, pressing me against his chest. He smelled good. His heart beat loudly, and reassuringly, beneath my ear. His arms were strong around me.

"I can't believe Eric challenged you to a singing duel." A picture of Eric and Jus at thirty paces with antique dueling pistols jumped into my mind. Their backup singers as seconds. Maybe that was more romantic. Also, scarier. Two guys singing over me was suddenly funny.

I grinned. "Eric usually doesn't pick a fight he can't win. He obviously had never heard you sing before. You were"—I searched for a word that adequately expressed what I felt—"amazing!"

I sighed, way happier than I should have been at being wrapped in Justin's arms and the thought of Jus putting Eric in his place. And I got a tingle all the way to my toes as I remembered Justin's sexy, smooth singing and the look in his eyes as he'd held me onstage.

"And neither had I." I snuggled into him. "I didn't know you could sing like that!"

"Singing a cappella is just another nerdy thing I used to do." He stroked my hair. "Since starting Flash I haven't had much time for it. I've been reduced to belting out a few songs now and again at happy hour with Riggins and Wylie for the staff's entertainment."

"You should sing more often." I meant it. "You handled Eric expertly tonight!" I couldn't keep the glee out of my voice. Eric deserved to have a hole punched in his ego, the loser. What had he been thinking? He hadn't, obviously. He'd probably just thought he could show off.

"Buying the losers a drink was epic!" I laughed. "Not that he needed one. He was already hammered."

"You're the one who handled things." Jus squeezed me and rested his chin on my head. "That song was perfect."

I would have liked to take credit for it. But I couldn't. "That was Sarah's doing."

He kissed the top of my head. "But you executed it perfectly. And you chose me." He sounded almost stupidly happy about that.

I almost made a flip remark that I had no choice but to choose him over Eric if we wanted to make our marriage look real. I bit my tongue just in time. Why burst his bubble? Because I wasn't sure now that I wouldn't have chosen him anyway. Eric could be such a douche.

"And I know how much you're embarrassed to sing in public," Jus said into my hair.

I flashed back to college and a memory of him asking me to come sing with him at open mic night in the student lounge. I'd always refused, brushing him off by saying I didn't sing. Which was true. It was sweet of him to remember that now. But it made me nearly squirm with guilt. It had been an *excuse* not to go out with him as much as anything. I was a bad, superficial person.

If I'd taken him up on it, I would have known what a gorgeous singing voice he had.

"Kay, I—" His voice wavered.

I pulled back so I could look him in the eye. He faltered, looking so adorably nervous. I recognized that expression. "You want sex again!"

I laughed. "Savagely beat a girl's ex in a brutal singing duel, risking vocal cords and public humiliation, and you think she owes you, is that it? You're expecting some gratitude!"

His timid smile froze, no longer reaching his eyes.

What had I said?

"Yeah." He looked sheepish. "I want sex. I always want sex." I couldn't tell if he was being sarcastic. He cleared his throat. "But I was actually about to ask you to come with me on my usual visit to the children's hospital tomorrow."

I answered quickly. "That's a bit of a non sequitur. But I'd love to."

He nodded. "Good. I'll introduce you to some of the people you need to know."

I saw past his subterfuge. That nervousness wasn't brought on by asking me to go to the hospital with him. "So you *don't* want sex?" I teased.

"I didn't say that." His eyes became dark and wide. "Are you offering?"

"Okay, big boy, don't play coy with me. I might be. Since you defended my honor with my big, bad ex. But you're going to have to sing to me. Something highly romantic and seductive."

He started singing "Never Gonna Give You Up" again, looking deep into my eyes in that intense way he had.

I reached up and stroked his beard, then took his hand and pulled him toward the bedroom.

CHAPTER TWO

Justin

Perched over Kay when she was naked beneath me was my favorite view of her. Although you could say when she was naked and riding me, her hair streaming over her bouncing breasts, was a close second. When we made love, and she was climbing toward climax, she got a dreamy, ecstatic expression. Her eyes half closed. Her lips gently parted. Her neck arched as she curved up to meet me.

"Harder, Jus. Harder, harder, *harder*." Her words came on gusts of sweet breaths.

The air conditioning kicked on, blowing her hair gently, teasing my nose with the scent of her.

We clenched hands, mine pressed down on hers, her arms at right angles showing off her sleek biceps. Her hair fanned out over the pillow. I couldn't stop looking at her, hoping I had this view at my disposal forever.

She gasped. And moaned softly. I would have done anything to please her. At that moment, while I was hanging on and trying not to come too early—which was a Herculean feat, believe me—I could look at her and *almost* believe she loved me. At least she wanted me. That was a good first step.

It was her mission to turn me into a skilled lover. So when I went on with my life without her, I would be a playboy billionaire? Someone more like Lazer? Damn, Lazer.

I laughed at the thought of her teaching me the ways of lovemaking, resisting the urge to call her coach. And reveled in my victory when I made her forget she was supposed to be critiquing my moves.

It was *my* mission to get her to fall in love with me using any means possible. As they say, all's fair in love and war. If I was doing my damnedest to make the sex between us unforgettable, who could blame me? If I secretly studied modern-day versions of the *Kama Sutra* and read online articles on men's health about how to find G-spots, maybe I could win her over.

Now I just had to get up the nerve to ask her to let me slide my fingers into her and tease her until I found it. So I knew what I was aiming for when I went in with my dick. If she had one of the famed, elusive G-spots, I was damn well eventually going to find it.

I fantasized about breaking away from Flash for a few weeks and sweeping her off to some romantic locale where all we had to do was screw.

With every thrust, I attempted to drive all thoughts of Eric so far out of her head she'd barely remember she'd ever known him. If she ever thought about him later, his skills in bed would pale by comparison to mine, as weak as his voice was against the strength of mine. I wanted him to lose every duel with me.

Damn, I tried hard. I tried hard to listen, to learn, to be as sensitive as I could to her needs. If Eric ran true to course, he was as selfish in bed as he was in the rest of the relationship.

She wanted it harder, so I gave it to her, to the best of my ability. Trying to angle against the odds in this position and hit the right spot. I paid attention. Shit, I paid attention to every detail of her.

I think she saw me like an eager puppy. But I was much more. I was the guy who loved her and everything about her, down to the imperfections that made her real.

I was in love, totally blinded by it. To me, she was the most gorgeous woman on the planet. My private centerfold. Even her flaws were beautiful and perfect. She had a scar on her left knee. Silvery, fine stretch marks on her breasts from puberty. Those breasts must have come on quickly. I can't tell you how sorry I was I missed their development. Not that the skinny boy me would have ever had a shot at seeing them like I did now.

Her figure was perfection, even if her hips were slightly out of proportion with the slenderness of the rest of her. I liked big-hipped women. Someday when we were old and gray together, she would be an old lady pear. And I would be an old guy apple. And I'd still think she was beautiful.

I thrust deeper, feeling myself crashing toward the cliff of climax.

Her breath caught. She moaned. She closed her eyes and gasped. She squeezed my hands until my rings dug into my flesh, then she arched up and cried out. Just an utterance. Not a word.

Someday, I vowed silently, *she will cry out my name.*

I let myself go. Let the waves crash and crash and crash until I shuddered and buried my face in her neck. And bit my tongue to keep from saying what was in my heart.

When it was over for both of us, I collapsed next to her in the softest sheets my money could buy. Breathing hard. Sweaty with sex. Wishing like hell I was as athletic and macho as my brothers. As suave as Lazer. As experienced as she needed me to be.

Waiting in the hum of the air conditioning for words she wasn't ready to speak. Desperate to break the silence and tell her how I felt. Watching her with a hunger that burned deep inside me, looking for a ghost of hope. Longing for the normalness of holding the woman I loved in my arms after being blown away with the force of making love to her and saying *I love you* to each other.

I flopped my arm over my forehead and lay on my back, looking at the ceiling, letting the lights of the city wash over us as I caught my breath. Riding high on the pleasure. Hiding my disappointment at her silence.

She turned toward me and smiled her slow, sated, sexy smile. Ran her fingers over my naked chest until I shivered with pleasure. Smiling because she liked teasing me with her touch. She wanted another literal rise out of me. And she was about to get it.

I wanted more. Four simple words: *I love you, Jus.*

I wanted to say, *I love you, Kay.* And not worry about recrimination. Or seeing her face fall. Or the panicked look while she frantically tried to let me down easy. Or say, *Oh, Jus,* with that pitying look in her eyes, like I was still that nerdy, hopeful guy, *I'm sorry I gave you the wrong impression. This is just sex.*

I couldn't risk scaring her off. I needed her in too many ways. I wanted to keep making love to her. I couldn't stand the thought of her leaving. Or the strain of tiptoeing around each other.

I'd almost blown it and blurted it out when we first got home. It was just a damn good thing she'd cut me off, thinking I was about to ask for sex. A damn good thing.

Even so, I smiled. Because it was impossible not to. I was still that happy. "So, how was it, coach?" It slipped out. I couldn't help it. "How did I do?"

"Coach?" She laughed.

"Isn't that what you are?"

She leaned up on one elbow, her head on her hand. "Maybe. But you know, it's gauche to ask."

"Not when you're asking your coach. Coaches give advice on technique."

"Do they?" She seemed amused.

I nodded, probably too eagerly.

"You really want to know?" She ran the back of her fingers over my beard.

I nodded.

"Solid B."

My face fell. "B?" I was stunned. "Harsh. I put everything I had into it."

She laughed again, still teasing me. But it was more like torment. "You get an A for effort, Jus. You always get an A for effort. And enthusiasm. But you're still a novice. We weren't fighting against each other like two cats in bag. But our rhythm isn't exactly smooth and in tune yet. Anyway, I can't give you an A so early in our year together. You'll get a big head and stop trying."

"Ah." I nodded, trying to keep my bravado up. "You're one of those kind of graders. You don't give top scores until the end of the semester. So you can prove I've learned something at your hands."

She cupped my face. "Oh, you've learned plenty already."

"Out of curiosity, what does a guy have to do to get top marks?"

"Be creative. You have to surprise me. Top students go above and beyond." She gave my face a playful tap and looked past me out the glass wall to the view of the city. "You have one thing going for you. It's totally hot making love with no curtains. Thrilling, like people could see us. But safe, because you know they can't."

She slid out of bed and walked to the window, where she stood, silhouetted against the city. I sat up, about to join her when she turned and headed toward the bathroom.

Someday, I would make love to her standing, pressed against that glass. And she would happily give me my A plus. I wasn't the kind of student who ever got anything less.

Kayla

Justin's BMW was sleek and showy and drew attention when he parked it in the children's hospital's maze of a parking lot. He zipped into a tiny, regular spot, apparently unconcerned about door dings. I generally didn't care much about cars, other than that they were comfortable, clean, and ran without incident. I would just as soon have driven a middle-class vehicle. Status models made me nervous. The thought of someone putting a dent in its expensive body gave me horror shivers. I wasn't used to having so much money that I didn't care about my nice things getting damaged, even superficially. It was a defect of mine that I liked to keep my nice things nice. I was almost OCD about it.

Jus had brought a Flashionista backpack from work. He threw it over his shoulder and took my hand as we walked across the parking garage to the sky bridge in the early afternoon. On with the show! After less than two weeks, it was amazing how easily we fell into our public role of couple in love. How smoothly our hands interlocked now without fumbling. How well we fit together and walked in step.

Jus beamed. He was so upbeat most of the time now it was hard not to smile with him. He amused me in so many ways. Like wanting to be graded on his lovemaking and calling me coach. He was insatiable and eager to please. It was adorable. Walking into the hospital, he had that same joyful look like after we made love. And an excited bounce in his step.

During the drive over, he'd warned me how hard it was to see the sick and suffering children. He'd prepped me with stories that could break the most hardened heart. And yet he'd been genuinely eager to see the kids. He took a deep breath. "Ready?"

He was so cute when he grinned like that, ready to save the world. Or at least as many sick children as he could.

I smiled at him. "Lead the way."

We met with the business development head, Brenda Cole. She was in charge of fundraising and charitable donations. And as far as I could tell, shepherding major donors around and treating them like VIPs. I put her at around forty. She was personable, in the way fundraisers are. A true politician. Pleasant. She and Jus seemed to know each other well.

She gave us the tour of the facilities, though it was really for me. Jus knew his way around like an insider. She and Jus shared inside jokes and stories. It was apparent they were old friends. I hadn't been aware Jus had such a long history with the hospital. I mean, how long could it be? He was only twenty-one. But apparently he and Riggins had been donating to it from the very meager beginnings of Flash.

Jus, as always, had a soft spot for children and underdogs. Especially children who were made fun of for being different. He stood up for anyone who was bullied. Which also explained why Jus and Flash supported the domestic violence shelters.

Brenda made a show of pointing out equipment and treatments the money from Flashionista and Justin's personal accounts had made possible. I'd had no idea how generous Jus was. The money seemed to matter very little to him, except in what it could do for the children and their families.

I thought, then, again, that I had "married" a good guy. Which was so counter to the guys I chose on my own.

Brenda introduced me to a succession of doctors and nurses who threw out terms like cardiomyopathy—dilated, hypertrophic, and restrictive. As if I knew the difference. As if I knew what cardiomyopathy was, other than a guess it had to do with the heart. I lost track of names. The doctors became a blur of white coats and medical terms. But Jus seemed to keep the doctors and the medical terms straight. And even understand them.

At the end of the tour, Brenda got me in touch with her highly capable staff and told me to contact them for whatever help I needed. They were at my disposal.

Finally, she smiled at Jus. "I'm sure you're eager to see the kids." She paused and rested a hand gently in his arm. "Sophia's back."

Jus muttered something beneath his breath about life not being fair and children with the biggest hearts having the worst ones. "How bad is it this time?"

Brenda stared at him silently.

"Yeah. Right. Privacy laws. You can't tell me." He looked through an open hospital room door, through an empty room, and out a window, trying to compose himself. "There's enough money in the benevolent fund to cover her treatment?"

Brenda nodded. "Come see her. She's eagerly expecting you. She's been talking about nothing else all morning."

"Is Vicki with her?"

"Only leaves Sophia's side when she has to. Which doesn't leave much for her job." Brenda pushed a double door open and led us to the cardiac care ward. "This way. Room 322."

We walked past a bustling nurses' station. A hospital is always a hospital, and smells like one. This one was brightly decorated for children, the walls covered with cartoon murals. But at its core it smelled like disinfectant and medicine. And both hope and despair. Nothing disguised that.

Brenda led us to a station to scrub up. In this area of the cardiac ward, children were particularly susceptible to airborne diseases.

"No need to gown up this time. Assuming you're both completely healthy? None of you have been exposed to anyone who might have Ebola or anything like that?" She raised an eyebrow in question.

Jus and I shook our heads.

Brenda smiled. "Good! I'd hate to disappoint a little girl today." Brenda stopped and knocked on the partially open door to a private room. "Sophia? Are you home? You have a visitor!"

A child's voice squealed from behind the privacy curtain. "Is it Justin?"

"It just might be. Shall I let him in and you can see for yourself?" Brenda led us into the room around the privacy curtain.

A slender, underdeveloped little girl with a distended stomach lay propped up in bed, surrounded by a menagerie of stuffed animals. She was so small. She couldn't have been more than three or four. She had a mop of curly brown hair and wide brown eyes that looked too large for her face. At the sight of Jus, her face lit up, transforming her into a loveable imp.

Justin's face lit up, too.

She held her arms out to him. "Squishy, squeezy hug!"

"Are you sure you're up for that? Last time I nearly squeezed the stuffing out of you!" He pulled her into a hug, rubbing her cheek with his beard while she giggled wildly and screamed at him to stop whiskering her. But when he tried to pull away, the little girl clung to him.

"I think you're squeezing the stuffing out of *me* this time!" he said.

She finally released him, totally ignoring both Brenda and me.

"Your beard is different." She frowned and ran a small hand through his hair. "You cut your hair!" She made a pouty face so serious and flirtatious I almost laughed.

"I did. Do you like my new look?" He held her gaze.

"The jury's out," she said, sounding terribly grown-up, probably imitating her mom. Who was nowhere to be seen.

Justin's answering laugh was deep and rich. "Where's your mom?"

"Getting a coffee. What did you bring me?" The girl reached for the backpack hung over Justin's shoulder.

"You are such an eager, greedy little thing!" He was still grinning as he slid the backpack off and set it on the bed. "Do you have Dolly with you?"

The girl rolled her eyes in an exaggerated way, shook her head, and made a grown-up sound of disgust. I wondered if her mom sounded like that, too. "Duh." She pulled a doll out from beneath the covers. It had apparently been lying in bed next to her.

Jus laughed, unzipped the backpack, and pulled out two pairs of sparkly pink pajamas, one sized for a doll, the other for the girl.

Her eyes went wide. She clapped as he handed them over.

He held a finger to his lips. "Shhhh. You can't tell anyone about these. They're brand new and exclusive to Flash. This is an advance sample. No one else has them yet. You'll be the first. Not only in Seattle, but the entire world."

The girl was already pulling the clothes off her doll and dressing her in the pajamas. "Dolly and me are going to look so pretty! Like twins!"

Brenda put a hand on my shoulder and whispered in my ear, "I'll leave you now. Justin knows his way around. It was nice meeting you. I expect we'll be seeing a lot of you now." She gave my shoulder a friendly squeeze and disappeared behind the privacy curtain and out the door.

Jus had been admiring Dolly in her new clothes. He stopped the girl just as she was about to peel off her shirt and change, too. "Hold on there a minute. I'm a boy. You can't change like that in front of me." He shielded his eyes comically.

She frowned and gave Jus a look like he was stupid or something. "I change in front of Dr. Nate all the time."

"Doctors are different," Jus said, calmly. "They have to see body parts so they can make them better."

The little girl rolled her eyes again. "You are so lame. Turn your back."

Jus laughed and stood. "I'll stand on the other side of the curtain. You call me when you're ready."

We heard rustling and some cute grunting.

"Having trouble?"

"No!" She sounded indignant. "I got it! I'm ready!"

Jus took my hand and pulled me with him around the curtain.

"Ta-da!" The girl held her arms up and out.

"You look beautiful!" Jus said in that adorable voice he used to tell me the same thing. The voice that actually made a girl feel the way he saw her.

The little girl's beam of happiness turned into a frown as her gaze slid to our clasped hands. Holding hands in public was becoming automatic.

"Who's *she*?" Her voice and face turned to thunder, startling in one so small with so little energy. She was in a pique of little girl jealousy.

"This is my new wife, Kayla." I swore his voice caught on the words. "Kayla, Sophia."

"I'm happy to meet you!" As I reached out my free hand to shake hers, Sophia recoiled and glared at me.

She shook her head vehemently. "No! No, you can't! You can't have a wife. You promised!" If she'd been standing up, she would have stamped her feet. Because she was lying in bed, she had to resort to pounding her pillow with her tiny fist in an impotent show of rage and displeasure. "*I* was going to marry you when I grew up! Remember, silly face?"

Justin's face softened. He hesitated. "Sorry, Sophia. You won't be grown up for a long time. I'll be an old man by then and you won't want me." He grinned at me. "But you're going to love Kayla as much as I do."

My heart did an odd little flip. Love me? How easily and casually he tossed the phrase around in public.

"She knows all about hair and makeup and fashion," he continued. "All those things you love."

Sophia's face twisted into a grotesque, exaggerated frown. Her little lips puckered. "I don't like her. You were supposed to marry Mommy until I got old. Then I would marry you."

"Who's supposed to marry me?" A slender woman, an older, healthier version of Sophia, pulled back the privacy curtain and stepped inside it, carrying a paper cup of cafeteria coffee. "Oh! Justin!" She flushed.

"Vicki!" He released my hand and hugged her.

From her bed, Sophia flashed me a smug smile. I realized that mama bear had just arrived. Clearly, Sophia was misguided in her beliefs about what her mom could and couldn't do.

Vicki was young. Much younger than I imagined. Had I imagined? I guess I involuntarily had. And I'd been picturing someone more my own parents' age, though that was silly. Because they were parents of a grown daughter, not a preschooler. But it was automatic, wasn't it, to imagine parents being, well, an advanced, experienced parental age?

I would have been surprised if Vicki was as old as I was, though she looked worn with worry. When Jus introduced us, I felt the slight chill of Vicki's disappointment. Had she been hoping to catch Jus, too? Was I the only girl in the world between the ages of three and ninety-three who'd been immune to his charms? Or did she see Jus as a way to provide for her sick child? Could I blame her for that?

Vicki was pretty in a hard, life-worn sort of way. Her face was young and smooth and covered with too much makeup. She would have looked younger and fresher with less. The look in her eyes was old, and almost afraid of getting older. I supposed having a sick child did that to a person. I took it there was no daddy in the picture. And in at least Sophia's mind, Jus was a good candidate.

Vicki shook my hand and sang Justin's praises, wishing us both happiness. "This is a surprise." Her gaze darted between us, landing on Jus. "I didn't know you were serious about someone. Not that it's my business."

"Well, why not?" Jus laughed, but he looked almost embarrassed. "It seems to be everybody else's. It's been all over the news since it happened."

"Oh? Well..." Vicki cleared her throat. "Sophia and I don't watch much except Nickelodeon."

Jus grinned. "That explains it. I don't think it was announced there."

"You'll have to excuse Sophia." Vicki gave her daughter a maternal look full of love and scolding. "She has confused ideas about marriage."

"I do not!" Sophia crossed her arms and frowned. "Justin is still going to marry me when I grow up." Her face softened as her mom gently sat on the bed next to her. "You can marry Mommy first if you want," she said in a completely gracious tone.

I was trying hard not to laugh or smirk. I had to put my hand over my mouth. "He's going to have to get rid of me first," I said, slyly.

Wait a year! Then he'll be free. And then, *No!* I felt the unexpected revulsion over the thought of losing him as much as I heard the word echo in my mind. The force of that "no" startled me. I was getting more and more possessive of Jus. Which was such a *bad* idea. Mom had always said I had grabby hands, always wanting to keep things to myself and not share.

"Oh, Sophia!" Vicki glanced at me. "Just ignore her. She'll get over it." Vicki tousled her daughter's mop of curly hair. "She's confused in that way little girls have of thinking they're going to grow up and marry Daddy."

Jus laughed. Nervously, I thought. He sat on the other side of Sophia's bed and asked Vicki how they'd been. Only in more detailed nuances than a simple

"What's up?" sort of thing. He was Jus. He remembered every little detail about everyone and everything.

Vicki blossomed under his attention and launched into another one of those discussions consisting mostly of medical terms and references to Sophia going to kindergarten in the fall.

I could see where Vicki could get the wrong impression about Justin's interest in her. Like I had at Mom and Dad's when I thought Jus had been stalking me. He was exceptional with his skill to remember personal details. And in Vicki's case, I believed she would have welcomed his attention. She'd read more into it than was there.

And, actually, bad person that I was, I felt a tiny stab of jealousy over how well Sophia and Vicki seemed to know Jus. And how much he seemed to care about them. And how, sitting on either side of Sophia, they almost looked like a couple. One could imagine they were, anyway. And I was standing there, the outsider.

As if he'd read my mind, Jus pulled me close and dragged me into the conversation. "Kay is going to take over our big annual sample sale and fundraising gala for the hospital this year." He beamed. Yes, actually beamed.

I felt myself nearly blush under his praise. And there was a look in his eyes, a searching look. Other than that, he played the part of a young groom in love almost too well.

Vicki was studying me, too. I wondered if we were fooling her. She seemed so wary and suspicious. So I did something I shouldn't have. I ran my hand through

Justin's hair, caressed his cheek, and leaned down to give him a soft, sweet kiss on the lips.

If he was startled, he didn't show it. He kissed me back and grinned almost wolfishly at me.

"Jus is almost insanely proud of me." I flashed him a flirty smile. "But I have big plans for it."

I could feel Vicki looking at me in my carefully picked out boutique clothes and jewelry from Flash. I could also swear I could read her mind. And she was thinking I wasn't good enough for Jus.

Sophia looked at me and just blurted out, "You're pretty!"

It seemed so out of the blue and like such a complete change of heart. We all laughed.

Sophia yawned and looked suddenly pale and worn out. Not that she'd been particularly energetic. Not in the way some of my former coworkers' children were. Vicki's face took on a look of alarm. I felt that chill that meant it was time for us to leave.

Jus felt it, too. "We should be going." He patted his backpack. "I have other gifts to distribute."

Sophia gave him a gigantic hug that must have zapped the rest of her strength. "Don't go!"

Jus had to pry her loose again. "I'll be back to visit you another time."

"When I get my new heart?" She looked at him with wondering, hopeful eyes.

I went cold.

Vicki blinked back a tear. Jus just winked at her. "Way before then!"

Later, as we walked back to the car after visiting dozens more sick children, I asked Jus about Sophia. "What's wrong with her heart?"

"Dilated cardiomyopathy."

I frowned, remembering one of the doctors mentioning it and something about forty to fifty percent five-year survival rates. "She's not going to grow up, is she?"

Jus looked away. But not before I caught a glimpse of a tear in his eye. "Without a new heart? Probably not." He paused. "And how can you wish for that when it means some other five-year-old has to die?"

I squeezed Justin's hand and felt myself falling a little bit in love with him. How could you not love a guy who cares so much?

CHAPTER THREE

Kayla

On Friday morning, I got up with surprisingly few butterflies in my stomach and a big dose of excitement. Today was my first official solo TV interview as Justin's wife. I was psyched.

Jus was up early, as usual, and sitting at the breakfast counter finishing a glass of freshly squeezed orange juice. While multitasking on his phone. Which I swore was almost surgically attached to him. When I walked into the room, he turned to look at me over his shoulder. His eyes lit up. He spun his barstool around so I could stand between his legs.

As I bent to kiss his uplifted face, he cupped my butt. Right in front of Magda. Who was busy in the kitchen on the other side of the counter. Jus hugged me enthusiastically and nuzzled his head into my breasts. Which he was fond of doing.

He swept a lock of hair behind my ear, wearing a grin that wouldn't quit. Jus always looked so damned happy when we had an audience. We'd fallen into the role of happy couple so easily. It was hard to resist that grin and not smile back.

From the kitchen, Magda smiled knowingly at us, as if she approved, and turned away.

"Happy two-week anniversary!" Jus gave me another quick kiss. If the way he was grabbing me was any indication, he wanted way more than kissing.

"Two weeks already! Wow! Are we oldly-weds now?" I ran my fingers through his hair, smoothing out an errant lock. "Happy anniversary to you, too, babe."

I found it amusing, and sweet, that he was celebrating our weekly anniversaries.

He handed me a jewelry box almost too nonchalantly. "I was going to give you this tonight at dinner." His eyes sparkled. "But then I thought you'd want to wear it on the show. Go ahead. Open it."

I bit my lip. "I didn't know this was a gift-giving holiday. I didn't get you anything—"

"Don't sweat it! I just saw this and thought you'd like it. Open it!"

"You are so impatient!" I pulled the bow off the box. When I opened the lid, I gasped. The most beautiful diamond tennis bracelet sparkled out at me. "Jus—"

I almost said it was too much. I couldn't accept it.

He put a finger to my lips to silence my protest. "Let me help you put it on." He put it on my wrist and fastened the clasp so smoothly, I wondered if he'd practiced.

"Thank you." I kissed him again. I told myself it was expected. But, deep down, I wanted to kiss him. More and more often.

"Do you have everything you need for the show? Did Marla make sure you have the giveaways for the audience? Of course, they're only crystal, not diamonds."

I nodded. "Andrea picked them up yesterday while we were at the hospital. Andrea is amazing! So efficient, calm, and competent. I think she's trying to impress Lazer."

A nearly imperceptible wrinkle formed between Justin's eyes. Lazer lending me an assistant was a sore spot with him. "Yeah. *Everyone* tries to impress Lazer."

By everyone, I assumed he meant me.

"A future permanent position for Andrea is on the line." I ignored his dig and tried not to sound too defensive.

Jus looked immediately sorry for bringing it up and gave me a playful pat on the butt. "Just watch yourself around her. I'm sure she reports everything back to Lazer. We have a spy in our midst!" He made a joke out of it. But he was serious.

I knew enough to keep my mouth shut. And keep our game on.

"Wish I could make it to the show."

I shook my head. "If you did, you would probably be the *only* guy in the audience. Sunshine Sheri's demographic skews heavily female. And as Sheri's assistant described this episode to me, it's a summer wedding theme. Like Sheri is fond of doing. I'm supposedly the expert and will be tasting wedding cake samples and giving tips." I shook my head. "As if I know anything about planning a wedding! We eloped."

Magda glanced over at us.

"You have great taste and you know delicious cake when you eat it—what more do you need?" Jus said with obvious pride.

I shook my head at him.

"I'm still sorry to miss it. I'm set up to record it. Break a leg!" He gently rubbed my arm.

"I don't think you tell interviewees to break legs," I said.

He winked, giving me a look that made my heart melt. It was so damned full of love and happiness. How the hell did he put that on? He never looked at me like that when no one was around. I was beginning to imagine I was hallucinating it. A desperate woman thirsty for love? Was I becoming one of those decoy brides who actually fell in love with her husband? And looked for whatever signs and hope she could find?

It would serve me right, I supposed. But at other times I wondered if all this pretending to be in love had simply gone to my head. Could my heart actually be starting to think it was real?

Jus glanced at his phone. "Shit! I have to be going." He downed the rest of his orange juice.

I walked him to the door.

He hesitated.

"Yes?" I said.

He looked so damnably nervous and adorable. "Mom's been texting. Begging me, coercing me, using all her motherly guilt-inducing tactics, to bring you to Naples for the last of the rugby season. She wants us to spend a few days with them before they finish their last summer rugby tournament. Meet Dad and my brothers. See the family biz in action."

He skimmed my arm with the backs of his fingers, looking at the floor. And then at me apologetically from beneath his lashes. "It will be trial by fire. But it's *not* a bad idea. We could take a few extra days and go down the Amalfi Coast. Make a mini-honeymoon out of it. Before the craziness of the fall shopping and the run-up to the Christmas season. Once fall hits, it's chaos at Flash until the mid-January retail dead zone."

He was nervous about trying to convince me to go to Italy with him? Was he kidding? I'd always wanted to go to the Amalfi Coast. Even if it meant dealing with his family in Naples first. "Yes."

He hesitated like he was only halfway through a prepared speech. "Really? Naples is a dirty city. And my brothers will give us both a ton of shit."

I nodded. "Going to Italy is on my list."

His face relaxed. "We could stop by Milan on the way. Check out a few of the Italian designers Flash has been eyeing. I could use your opinion."

I grabbed his arm. "I would absolutely love that!"

He smiled. "Great. I was thinking we'd take a private jet to Milan. From there to Genoa. On to Naples for a few. Then hire a car down the coast. Or rent a yacht for day or two."

I was already dreaming about it. A honeymoon was a great idea. It added authenticity to our marriage. "Sounds wonderful to me!"

His answering grin was positively boyish and charming. "We'll do it, then! I'll text Mom and get Ophie to make the arrangements and get back to you." He gave me a parting kiss and was finally out the door before I could protest.

Ophie? That wasn't going to go over well.

Magda had been bustling around, conspicuously busy and *not* listening to our conversation. She'd been bursting to say something all morning. Once Jus was gone, she let loose. "Mr. Jus never does interviews!"

I couldn't tell whether she was condemning him or me or what. But I was glad she'd been concentrating on the interview and not our vacation.

"He should. He really should!" I said with that burst-of-pride voice. Where had it come from? "He would be fantastic at them! He shouldn't let Riggins hog all the spotlight all the time. You should have seen Jus at the hospital yesterday, Magda. He charmed everyone!"

Magda had been slowly warming to me day by day. Since I'd followed her advice and changed my name, I'd gotten on her good side. She smiled approvingly—at both my sentiment and the way I was gushing about Jus—and nodded. "That's what I say! But will he listen?"

I took a sip of coffee. "Are you sure you don't want to come backstage with me and that new personal assistant, Andrea, that Lazer sent over to help me? If you're lucky, you might get a chance to meet Sunshine Sheri." I singsonged the last bit, trying to entice her.

Magda brushed my suggestion aside. "No, thanks! I'll be much happier in the audience. But maybe I could just get her autograph *after* the show."

Sunshine Sheri was the affectionate nickname Seattle gave *Northwest Mornings* host Sheri Carmichael. She'd picked up the moniker when she'd begun her career as a weather girl during the record-breaking hot, dry Seattle June of 1992. I, of course, was barely born, so I didn't remember it. All this was according to her LinkedIn bio. Not the nickname bit. The part about the start of her career. The name stuck, in large part, because of her upbeat attitude and sunny smile.

Magda loved her and watched her daily morning show while she cleaned the penthouse and attended to her duties. She was something of a Sunshine Sheri fanatic. Since I'd gotten the interview, she'd worked Sheri any way she could work into conversation, subtly or, in most cases, obviously. It was getting pretty hilarious, really. I'd had no choice but to invite her along and get her a ticket in the studio audience.

Sheri was an aging star now, in TV terms, and relegated to the semi-popular morning show that did puff pieces, human interest, and public service announcements. She was the friendly, perky TV host talking to minor celebrities and locals of note. She did a weekly segment with a local gardening expert, cooking pieces with regionally known top chefs, that kind of thing. Going on her show was like being tossed a slow-pitch softball by someone who wanted you to get a home run.

There was no reason for nerves. How could anyone be afraid when they had Sheri to make them look good?

Three hours later, Sheri's makeup and wardrobe people did a last-minute touchup to me backstage while Sheri gave me a glowing introduction to her audience. "Ladies and gentlemen, I'm so pleased. The theme of today's show is one of my favorites—summer weddings! Well, it's June, so what else could we do?"

She flirted expertly with the audience. "Our special guest today is the summer bride of the season. Please welcome the new bride everyone is talking about. And every single Seattle girl wishes she were. Come on out, Kayla! Ladies and gentlemen—"

Gentlemen? I peered out at the crowd from backstage, looking for one. Were there any gentlemen? Or even any regular guys, gentlemanlike or not?

"I give you Mrs. Justin Green!" Sheri clapped.

That was my cue. One of Sheri's crew checked my mic a final time.

Andrea gave me a gentle push toward the stage. "You're on! Relax. You'll be great!"

I walked across the stage, smiling and waving to the studio audience while they applauded politely. Sheri's producer had given me a brief two days ago, asking me to dress like a guest at a summer wedding. The perfect outfit had come to mind immediately.

I was wearing my favorite, flirty little yellow dress I'd gotten off Flashionista shortly before we "got married." And a pair of spectacular platform sandals in nude with rhinestone bows that Jus had brought home for me from the merch buyers stock of samples specifically to wear on the show. The shoes were going to be featured on the Flash site this very day. We hoped me wearing them would be good for sales. I looked so much like the quintessential Flashionista girl. I could have stepped from the pages of their daily digital catalogue.

Sheri greeted me with a hug. "Look at you! Beautiful! Just like a young bride should be. Doesn't she look fabulous?" She turned to the audience for confirmation.

More applause.

I hadn't had a chance to meet Sheri before the show. Some last-minute emergency she had to attend to. Usually, at least in every show I'd seen, Sheri was dressed in something seasonally fun and stylish. Today, like me, she was dressed as a fashionable wedding guest. Flash's stylists had sent a selection of outfits over for Sheri. In exchange for a sponsor thanks at the end of the show. It had been my suggestion. The more advertising, the better.

I recognized the dress she was wearing as the most severe of the selection. We'd sent her everything from whimsical and flirty, to staid and traditional. Although the flared skirt of her dress gave it a fun air, she erred on the side of staid and traditional. To the point she could decently be confused for a newsroom anchor. Her hair was up in a severe, businesslike French twist. A few loose tendrils would have softened it. I itched to pull a few free. Even her lipstick was darker than usual.

She took a seat on the sofa and patted the place next to her, smiling brightly. I should have felt surprisingly at ease. Sheri had that bubbly, enthusiastic way that makes for good TV. But something felt off to me. I hoped she wasn't having a bad day.

As I smiled at the audience, Magda gave me a thumbs-up from the front row.

I had a communications minor and had done some work with the university's TV station, so I wasn't a complete neophyte. I knew all about sound bites and how words and quotes could be taken out of context. I was representing Flashionista and Jus as much as myself. So I was properly armed for battle. Not like it seemed like there was going to be one. Sheri was perfectly pleasant and always harmless. But I was ready for anything.

"Kayla, best wishes from all of us! You're the envy of every single girl in Seattle right now. Their inspiration. You came out of nowhere and snagged one of Seattle's most eligible, and richest, bachelors. I have it on good authority from a friend of mine, a confidential source, who works for the magazine that makes the yearly list of Seattle's hottest bachelors, that she's devastated. So much of her work down the drain now. Justin was going to be featured as one of Seattle's hottest men this September, right along with, shall we say"—Sheri winked—"several of his friends who've received the honor in past years. You've ruined her story." She paused.

Jus made the list? Really? Before I got my hands on him and prettied him up? That seemed like a stretch. Was I supposed to answer? Defend myself? I smiled and shrugged good-naturedly. "Love happens!"

Sheri nodded sagely. "Well, I think we can at least partly attribute Justin's new, hot look to you. Pictures of him since your marriage show a happy, well-groomed, *well*-dressed guy. Quite a difference from a few months ago. We're all dying to hear what it's like to go from rags to riches?"

I fixed a smile on my face. The little minx was trying to trap me and make me look like I went after Jus for his money. Who did she suddenly think she was? She'd turned into a Cokie Roberts clone, going for the journalistic kill and the inside story.

"I wasn't in rags." I kept my head high. "I come from an upper middle-class family. Mom's a lawyer. Dad's a doctor. I'm a young professional—"

"Who worked part time at a small, struggling men's underwear company." Sheri smiled at the audience as if letting them in on her inside joke. "Tighty whities, anyone? Was your desk full of samples of men's briefs?"

I opened my mouth to give a flippant remark, something along the lines of, *Oh, no! I give them to all my guy friends and one-night stands.* I caught a look of thunder on Magda's face and changed course just in time.

"I couldn't comment on whether my former employer is struggling or not. But it was a perfectly respectable first professional job. My degree is in business and fashion merchandising. It was a natural fit for my skills—"

"Going from struggling with men's briefs"—heavy on the innuendo—"to living in a gorgeous Bellevue penthouse with a 360-degree view of, well, everything!

The water, the mountains, downtown Seattle across Bellevue! You're looking down on everyone. No one can say you haven't come up in the world. Substantially come *up*."

"Yes, the penthouse is lovely. But money isn't everything. My apartment in West Seattle is in the heart of one of the hottest areas in Seattle, especially for my generation. I was surrounded by friends. I loved it there—"

"But it can't compare to now, can it? You're living like a princess. In the spotlight. Dressing in all the *best* clothes. Things regular woman can't afford." She leaned toward me with that serious journalist look on her face. Which was comical on her. Sunshine Sheri just wasn't the next Christiane Amanpour.

Inwardly, I sighed with relief. She'd just accidentally tossed me that soft pitch I'd been expecting. I smiled, genuinely happy to get another plug in. "Actually, *every* girl *can* afford to dress the way I do. That's the whole point of Flashionista. I bought this dress off the Flashionista site *before* I married Jus. Flashionista has prices to fit every girl's budget. *You* can dress like a princess, too—"

"Yes, yes, everyone loves Flash!" Sheri smiled too warmly. "That's what made Justin and his business partner Riggins billionaires, after all. They, *apparently*, know what women like." She put a little too much innuendo in her voice.

The live studio audience laughed. Everyone but Magda. She looked confused.

Sheri's eyes narrowed. She gave my arm a patronizing touch. "Before we get to the heart of our show and start tasting cakes and critiquing wedding attire, what everyone *really* wants to know is how you snagged such a determined bachelor?"

It was hard not to look startled by the question. "Jus is only twenty-one. I wouldn't call him a *determined* bachelor. The average guy my age doesn't get married until, what? Twenty-seven?" I stopped just short of saying Jus was still a baby.

"Maybe not in the *strictest* sense, but we have it on excellent authority that he wasn't seeing anyone. Wasn't even dating casually. Way too busy building Flashionista into one of Seattle's fastest-growing businesses. And then, there you were, his blushing bride, popping up out of nowhere!" She looked giddy.

Why was *I* on the spot here? Where was that cake?

"It wasn't *that* sudden." I had to force the quaver of anger out of my voice. My smile felt frozen on my face. *Be animated. Be happy! Be personable!*

"Jus and I have known each other for years. I'm sure you've done your research." A jab back at her. "We met in college. But Jus was, well, very young back then. He started college at sixteen."

I laughed, self-deprecatingly. "Yes. I am the older woman. I went to college at the usual age. He wasn't ready for a relationship then, and I was dating someone else. When we reconnected, we were both single. And ready for something serious. When you meet the right person, it feels right. We knew from almost the first minute we said hello that we belonged together. Why put off the inevitable?" I was getting a little indignant and trying not to let it show.

The audience gave a collective sigh. True love, wasn't it great?

I smiled into the camera and did an air kiss. "I love you, Jus." In that moment, I thought I meant it. My real life and my fantasy life were blending together.

The audience sighed.

"Who could resist Jus?" I said before Sheri could cut me off. "You've seen him, people. You know what I'm talking about. He's sweet, charming, thoughtful, super smart, and smoking hot!"

I turned to the audience and winked at them. "Sheri just said he was on the Seattle's Hottest Bachelor list for fall. So am I blinded by love and completely wrong?"

Whistles and hoots erupted, along with enthusiastic applause. Someone yelled, "I wouldn't kick him out of bed!"

The edges of Sheri's mouth curled very slightly into a snarl, hardly enough to notice unless you were paying close attention. Like I was. She was pissed I was taking over her show. And quashing her agenda.

"I was about to ask what attracted you to Justin." Her laugh was forced and sarcastic. "Now we know! We promised the audience tips about dressing as guests for different types of summer weddings. You put together some sample outfits for us. Are you ready for us to bring out the first ensemble?"

I nodded, and Sarah came out wearing an outfit appropriate for a beach wedding, including a pair of barefoot sandals. Sole-less shoes. I described the elements of the outfit, what made it such a good choice, and how much viewers could save by looking for deals on it and buying it at Flash.

As Sarah left the stage, Sheri clapped politely. "Tell us about your wedding, Kayla. What would have been appropriate attire for it?" Her question was barbed. Ouch.

Even though my heart stopped—how did I know what happened at Justin's wedding? Even he didn't remember—I kept smiling. Viewed in a certain light, it was kind of funny. I tried to keep it light. "We eloped on the spur of the moment. So I guess whatever you were wearing at the moment."

"Did you have guests at the wedding?"

"No." I was pretty confident about that.

I'd brought three more outfits with me. We went through the same routine with each, including the dress and shoes I was wearing. My diamond bracelet sparkled and caught the light as I gestured and pointed at each accessory and clothing element.

"That's a gorgeous diamond bracelet!" Sheri held out her hand. "Here. Let me see it." She took my hand in hers. "Fabulous."

I beamed. "Thank you. Jus gave it to me this morning for our two-week anniversary."

That got a sigh out of the audience.

Sheri dropped my hand. "Most new grooms can't afford such an expensive gift. What *is* it like living the life of a billionaire's wife? You quit your tighty-whitie job, didn't you?" Her gaze was piercing. Or trying to be. (Though, coming from Sunshine Sheri, it was a little funny ha-ha.) And her voice was heavy with accusation.

Wait a minute! I hadn't stolen from anyone. I took a deep breath and reached deep inside for suitable sound bites. I kept on smiling. "Living with Jus is a wonderful surprise every day. And I don't mean diamond bracelets. He treats me with respect and love. Better than any guy I've dated before. We have fun together. Any girl can have that with her guy. It's free, and yet it's priceless."

Sheri's nostrils flared gently. She was furious at being thwarted in whatever weird agenda she had. I was winning her audience. Which had been growing thin in recent months. And was rumored to be packed with staffers and people dragged in off the street. But was packed today with Justin's admirers. And possibly the hope of a free gift from Flash.

"And your job?"

"Yes, I did quit. I have so many friends, recent college grads, looking for work. Finding a professional job is a struggle for my generation. Better for my old job to go to one of them when I don't need it financially now." And I was about to be axed anyway, due to how bad the company was doing. But I didn't want to advertise the trouble my former employer was in. "I'm focusing my efforts on pro bono now, and volunteering and running some of Justin's charitable projects."

I launched into a brief description of the needs of the children's hospital and the good work they were doing.

"Wonderful," Sheri said.

What could she say without looking like a horrible bitch?

She broke for a brief commercial and completely ignored me as the staff set up for our cake-tasting display. I wandered into the crowd, shook hands, and answered questions. The ladies in the audience wanted to see my bracelet and were dying of curiosity about my wedding. I became the artful dodger, evading questions on the fly.

Sheri's assistant called me back up on stage to the display of wedding cakes and toppers that had been rolled in. And then we were back live.

Sheri introduced the cake segment. "Did you have a cake at your wedding? A reception?"

I laughed. "No. And no. It all happened too fast." I was purposefully vague.

Sheri made a pretty pout and sighed heavily. "So sad. You must be a different kind of girl not to want a dream wedding."

Not as different as she thought. I shrugged, feigning modesty. "It's the marriage that counts, not the ceremony."

Did I really say that? I was turning into a different kind of person.

"You deprived the city of a great deal. We were all hoping we could cover a fabulous, extravagant billionaire wedding." Sheri moved to the first cake, a three-tier beauty with a topper of a loving groom holding his bride up by the waist.

"Jus is extremely private," I said. "There wouldn't have been much to cover."

Sheri described the cake—a tuxedo cake—and handed me a cake knife and server. "Since you never got to cut a cake, will you do the honors?"

"Who says I never got to cut a cake?" I demonstrated my expertise.

We both tasted it and left it to her staff to hand out samples to the audience while we moved on to the next cake.

I stopped in front of it and held back a laugh. "Now this one has an interesting topper! It looks more like it belongs at a bridal shower or bachelorette party."

The bride and groom were grabbing each other's butts.

"You like that one?" Sheri's smile was vicious. "We'll give it to you as a parting gift."

"That's lovely of you." The bitch. "Jus will get a kick out this!" And he would.

"What is Justin like in private?" Sheri asked while we sampled the pink lemonade cake. "Give us a glimpse?"

"The same as he is in public—sweet and thoughtful. Totally adorable." Not as obviously in love with me as he put on for others. Was I a little bit jealous of the public us?

I launched into the story about Sophia and how Jus had sent flowers ahead to my parents. I found myself getting mushy, really believing my words.

"You really are madly in love with him?" Sheri's smile was laced with arsenic, sweet enough to kill.

"Yes. *Desperately.*" Did I look sincere enough? Would I have fooled the Great Pumpkin?

Sheri got a triumphant gleam in her eye. "And yet, just the other night, your ex, who you broke up with less than two weeks ago, got into a battle of the voices at a local bar. And fists very nearly flew." Sheri paused and looked at a screen in front of her as a video clip from that night popped up on a large screen behind us.

What the—

I collected myself. "Turn the volume on so we can hear Jus sing! His voice is totally sexy. He'll turn you into a fangirl." Did I sound like I had enough wifely pride? I surprised myself.

Sheri arched an eyebrow. "They don't look friendly."

I laughed it off. "The whole thing was just a joke! Two old college buddies who love to sing hamming it up and pretending to duel over me. Pranking each other. You know how guys can be." I rolled my eyes for effect.

The audience laughed.

"I clearly picked Jus. As Eric knew I would." Nice to get a jab at Eric in, too.

"You didn't have a bachelorette party. But what about the rumors about you and Lazer Grayson? Marry in haste, repent when you meet a hotter billionaire?"

I frowned, catching myself just in time before I blurted out, *What rumors?* I managed to shrug ever so slightly. "I'm not aware of any rumors. Lazer is a good friend to both of us."

Sheri's answering smile was perfectly wicked. "Yes, but the gossip mill reports you were a little too cozy with Lazer at the highly secretive EIEIO meeting just days after your marriage to Justin."

How would Sheri know about that? I didn't respond.

"And that Lazer commissioned a character of you to be put in a highly anticipated new video game he's heavily invested in."

A picture of the video game character me flashed on the monitor in front of me. The audience gasped.

"Is this how Lazer sees you?" Sheri said.

I brushed it off. "I have no idea how Lazer sees me. That's a video game character!"

I laughed. "How many fully clad, flat-chested, average-looking video game heroines have you seen?" I smiled sweetly. "Lazer wants his game to sell, so of course he's going to make sure all the characters in it are attractive."

Sheri's eyes lit up. "Are you saying you're attractive and that Lazer thinks so, too?"

"I'm saying that enhanced cartoon characterization of me is attractive. Lazer's artists are very good. And now Jus has a 'picture' of me he can be proud to put on his desk." I winked into the camera.

Sheri was getting testy. "How sweet."

How sarcastic.

"Did Justin have a bachelor party?"

Where was this leading? I hesitated. "No, of course not."

"Then what is this about?" Sheri's voice had a triumphant edge, as if she was about to skewer me with piece of investigative journalist genius.

She turned to look over her shoulder at the screen behind us. "This was taken just hours before the wedding. He's having drinks and looking cozy with a woman who isn't you."

Suddenly we were all staring at a picture of a woman who was obviously trying to be me—blond hair, probably a wig, about the same height, obviously heavier than I was. Wearing a pink dress, of all things. *Hot pink.* A shade Jus could see. So he had been right about that.

She was sitting on a barstool next to Jus at the hotel in Reno, quite clearly coming on to him. Her back was toward the camera, her face turned sideways so we could only see a partial profile, not enough to identify her, really. She was holding a margarita and invading his personal space.

My heart nosedived for my stomach. My mouth went dry. I tried hard not to let it pop open. A ball of anger flamed inside me. There was that awful ID-stealing bitch, probably wearing a dress she'd bought with *my* credit card. Dressed like me so she could use my ID and hit on my husband—

Wait, Jus wasn't my husband then. Okay, hit on the guy who'd had a crush on me in college. Fury nearly blinded me. And in fact, it probably saved me. That, and getting a glimpse of a stunned Magda in the front row. Turned out she was my ground in all this.

I had to save the situation, even as my heart pounded with an odd cocktail of fear, anger, and excitement. Where had Sheri gotten that picture? And was there any way Jus and I could use it to shut that thief down? Unfortunately, her face was mostly obscured.

I broke into a fabulous smile and clapped softly, trying to look as amused as possible. "Where in the world did you get that! Jus and I laughed so hard about that little incident, later.

"Women are always hitting on my husband. It's an occupational hazard of being a billionaire. That must have been taken while I was in the bathroom. Honestly! I leave him alone for a fraction of a second and another woman tries to snatch him!"

Which was the honest truth. I was in the bathroom. Puking my brains out in my hotel room.

I hitched my thumb toward the screen and kept smiling. *Smile and wave, Kay,* I told myself. *And make stuff up. Answer the question you wish you'd been asked.*

"I popped out for a second. When I came back, this overly done blond was hitting on Jus. Imagine!

"Jus said she moved in the instant the bathroom door closed behind my cute little butt. His words, not mine. Like the little opportunist had been ready to pounce, looking enough like me that she hoped Jus had a type and she was it." I winked at the audience, roping them in on my joke. "But Jus and I only had eyes for each other."

The audience had been on the edges of their seats and deathly silent. They exhaled as one and burst into a round of wild applause.

Sheri frowned and moved into a brief segment about honeymoons, bringing in a travel expert to talk about the pitfalls and joys of honeymoon travel.

After it was over, Sheri smiled artificially sweetly at me. "You didn't have a honeymoon? That's not very billionaire-like *or* romantic. You'll have to get Justin to take you somewhere fabulous for a late honeymoon."

"He's already making plans!" I felt defensive on his part. "He's taking me to Italy. To Milan and the Amalfi Coast."

Sheri's smile froze. I'd slipped away again.

We had a final commercial break and came back to the last segment—buying thank-you gifts for the bridal party. I'd brought a display of items the staff at Flash thought were perfect. I described the items, elaborating on exactly why they were the fantastic, thoughtful gifts to show your appreciation for the time, money, and effort your bridesmaids had put in. For them to remember your nuptials by.

As if I was on expert on *any* of this wedding stuff. I had, however, been a bridesmaid too many times and gotten stuff that was frankly crap. The final item I'd brought with me was a stunning silver and crystal bracelet that could be engraved and personalized. And looked way more expensive than it was, especially if you were lucky enough to get it in one of Flash's events.

I took the sample off the velvet bracelet display peg and put it on next to my diamond bracelet, holding out my jeweled wrist for the camera. "This is my favorite piece of the entire line. Look how pretty it looks, even next to my real diamonds! I love it so much I brought one for each of you! Bring them out, guys!"

The audience had been waiting for this. They erupted in applause as I waved the serving guys out. *Smile and wave, Kay. Smile and wave!*

"Compliments of Flashionista. Now you all can be Flashionista women, too!"

While the audience was distracted and putting on their bracelets, I glanced at Sheri. I had to find out how and where she got that photo.

CHAPTER FOUR

Kayla

On the way home in the car, Magda had turned from Sunshine Sheri super fan to major detractor.

"I can't believe she tried to make it look like Mr. Justin was unfaithful to you hours before your wedding!" She put a disdainful huff into her voice. "He's not the type to fool around! Before you, he didn't have a girlfriend. Or date."

Can you be unfaithful hours before an unplanned, impromptu wedding to a girl you've just reconnected with? That was one of those moral enigma questions someone with way more smarts than me would have to ponder.

I nodded. "Yeah. What was up with her? Her assistant apologized profusely. I think she's afraid of Jus and his connections and what they could do to Sheri's show if they chose. Sheri's evidently having some kind of midlife crisis where she thinks she needs to 'get serious' and leave a body of work that 'means something.' Like a hard-hitting piece on a billionaire's elopement? That doesn't even make sense!"

I tried to play it cool. But I was nervous and jumpy. Could Sheri have somehow found us out? I had to talk to Jus and tell him everything I'd learned. I'd been texting him like a crazy woman. But I had to veil everything. Send cryptic messages like, *Call me so I can tell you all about the show!*

Yeah, like that would set his alarm bells off. I looked like an excited media hound. I was relying on the sheer volume to tip him off.

At least I'd managed to beg Sheri's assistant to email me a copy of that damning picture of Jus with my ID-thieving wannabe me. Jus would know what to do with it. He'd use his mad computer skills to put a stop to things. In an odd way, I was excited that we finally had a picture of her to work from.

Magda sighed. "Sheri's shows have been getting—what's the word?—edgier! Yes, edgy lately. Not so light and fun like I like. But this was the first time she's been mean to a guest. On a show about love, too!

"If I had seen her act this mean way before, I would have warned you. Or Mr. Justin. Mr. Justin would never have let you go on that show then!"

I loved Magda's loyalty. But I almost laughed at the thought of Jus going all alpha dog on me and putting his foot down, forbidding me to go on the Sunshine Sheri show.

My phone rang. When I picked up, Britt was bubbling over with excitement. "I just got an offer from Flash! As a senior merch buyer." She rattled off the details, including a salary that Jus had been exceptionally generous with.

I felt the noose tightening. Complications were flying today. Britt at Flash. This could either be fantastic. Or the death of a beautiful friendship. I was in the proverbial rock and hard place spot. If Jus didn't give her a job, I was doomed. If he did, the jury was still out.

What happened when Jus and I broke up? Would Britt side with him because he was her big boss and figuratively signed her paychecks? Or with me, her longtime wronged friend? Would she last a year at Flash?

She'd just interviewed for the job on Tuesday. Jus had fast-tracked her. I made the appropriate supportive noises. Even going so far as to squeal in joy with her at her news. But deep down, I was worried. No, I was terrified.

When we got back to the penthouse, I gave Magda the rest of the day off. With the excuse Jus and I were going out to dinner, anyway. And the afternoon was too nice to waste indoors. She was having family over for a late dinner and was grateful to have more time to prepare.

Jus didn't reply to my texts. He was probably tied up in important meetings and had shut his phone off. Or had just become so engrossed in his programming that the outside world couldn't reach him. I'd noticed that about him. If he was deep in thought, I could call his name and he wouldn't hear me.

Sheri's assistant was true to her word. She emailed me the picture. Every time I looked at it I went cold and felt sick to my stomach, wondering if I could believe the story Sheri's assistant had told me. Or if the truth was the ID thief had sent it in. Was she threatening us again?

About seven, after I'd stewed for the entire day, Jus texted he was wrapping things up and sorry to be running late. Could I meet him at the restaurant for dinner? We'd planned to go to one of those Brazilian places where they gorge you to death with serving after serving of roasted meat. I wasn't a big meat eater, but Jus had been excited about it. And since I hadn't gotten him a two-week anniversary gift, relenting was the least I could do.

I almost cancelled on him. But then I figured, after that spectacle of a talk show, it wouldn't hurt our image to be seen happily out and about town. So in the spirit of Brazil, I changed into a tight red dress that showed off my butt, augmented by a butt-enhancer, since Brazilian fashion is all about the butt rather than the breasts, and put on another pair of platform sandals.

At the restaurant, Jus was apologetic. And couldn't stop staring at me. "Wow! I didn't know you had such a killer ass."

I shook my head and whispered, "You didn't? Maybe because your eyes don't usually go lower than my breasts."

He grinned devilishly. "Yeah, and I'm going to have to give that ass more attention next time."

I shook my head. "Look all you want. Just remember, it has a little help tonight from an enhanced foundation garment." I grinned.

He took my hand as the hostess showed us to our table. "How was the show? I've been so damned busy I haven't had time to watch it yet."

I took a deep breath as I was seated. All those texts evidently hadn't clued him in. I took my menu from the hostess and waited until she'd told us our server would be right with us and disappeared before I responded. "We need to talk about the show. In private. But let's just say it would help our image while we're out to look *very* happy together."

Which Jus took to mean PDA, and tons of it. And feeding me bits of meat from his plate. After two small servings, I was meated out. For being so slender, Jus put away a surprising amount of beef, chicken, lamb, sausage, and grilled pineapple, just to balance things out. Because, you know, you need your daily servings of fruit.

I heard a few murmurs emanating from the tables around us. We turned heads. People nodded and subtly pointed to us. We'd been recognized. The happy couple PR was good for us.

By the time we got home, Jus was buzzed and horny. I, however, was still full of the fear of that picture Sheri had shown. It was the first time I'd seen my thieving impersonator, and I was shaken up. Jus forgot the show was only for public consumption. When we were safely closed in the penthouse, he started kissing my neck and pressing me to him.

"Jus." I arched my neck away from him and braced my hands against his chest. "We need to talk. About the show."

"Later, Kay." He kissed my neck, his voice deep and full of seduction and good humor. "Right now I need another lesson in love."

I laughed. He could be so funny at the oddest times.

"You're laughing at a desperate man." He practically breathed the words into my ear. "I'm a good student. You won't be disappointed by my progress."

"Jus. We *need* to talk. There was a development on the show today."

He nuzzled my neck. I hated to throw cold water on his ardor, but I'd been desperate all day, too. With worry. "Sheri showed a picture of the identity thief and you together on her show."

He froze. "What did you say?"

I repeated it.

He let me go so fast I nearly toppled over. "No! How?"

I pulled my phone from my purse and showed him the emailed picture from Sheri's assistant. He went stark white.

I took his arm and led him to the sofa. He sat and took the phone from me and just stared at the picture in silence. His face clouded with fury. It was frightening. I'd never seen him look like that.

I sat next to him, leaning forward with my hands on my knees so I could see his downturned face. "Is it her? Is it that night?"

"Fuck. Yeah, it's her." He was trembling. With either fear or rage. I wasn't sure which was the better option at that point.

"FYI, she's wearing a pink dress. You were right about that."

He didn't see the humor in it. I made him watch the show on the mounted large-screen TV. We watched it together. I actually looked better than I thought. They always say TV adds ten pounds. Call me vain, and I probably am, but I didn't want to look like a fat cow.

I almost made a quip about needing popcorn while we watched my Seattle TV debut. But I was sure Jus wouldn't have appreciated my sense of humor. I'd had all day to digest the news. He was just getting started.

He was stonily, icily silent, concentrating with an unreadable look on his face. When it was over, he flipped it off. "How did you get the picture on your phone?"

I explained how I'd talked to Sheri's assistant. "She told me Sheri has been on a rant about her show's ratings falling. And being middle-aged and needing more. Sheri wanted to do something more serious on our wedding. So she went digging for scandal. Her staff had almost given up when they found a paparazzi wannabe who'd recognized you from your many trips to the Reno facility. I guess you've been written up in the paper down there for bringing good jobs to town." I glanced at Jus. He was like a statue.

"He'd snapped the picture and hung on to it, hoping it would be worth something. When he sold it to her, he claimed he'd snapped it on the same date as our purported wedding, just hours before. And had the time stamp to prove it. Sheri was only too happy to have anything on you. I don't think she knows what's going on. But what if she keeps digging? What if she finds this woman before we do?"

We sat in silence. I didn't interrupt Justin's thoughts.

Finally, he sighed. "My PI is still working the case. This picture could be the break he needs to find her. If he circulates it..."

"He'll have to be *extremely* discreet." I didn't like this at all. "What if she spooks easily? If she gets wind we're looking for her, she could bolt—"

"He's the best in the business." Jus leaned back against the sofa. Finally, he turned and looked at me. "Dex and I coded a piece of facial-recognition software together in college. I can tweak it to see if I can find her." He tapped my phone. "That won't be easy, either. We only have a partial view of her face. And she's clearly in disguise."

I nodded, feeling miserable for both of us.

"Shit!" He took another deep breath. "Wall Street is analyzing our midyear numbers right now and making projections. They've been overly optimistic, in my opinion. Thinking we're going to track the success and growth rate of Amazon. We're making money, good money. But it won't matter. If we miss our targets, they'll downgrade our stock. If a scandal like this breaks, they'll really downgrade us."

He frowned. "We have to stop her." He took my hand. "If we let him in on this, Dex could help. He knows the software as well as I do."

"No!" I shook my head. "The PI—"

"Dex has a unique way of looking at things. I could use his brainpower. And he can keep his mouth shut."

Jus had the most to lose here. I had no right, really, to interfere with what he thought was the right thing to do. I swallowed hard. He was right about Dex. He *could* keep a secret.

I nodded. "Okay." But I still wasn't certain. "Just so you know, I'll never hear the end of it from Dex. It's a huge sacrifice on my part."

"Are you angling for more money? Don't tell me you're going to blackmail me, too?" He was so darn cute as he squeezed my hand. "Something doesn't make sense—why did the ID thief contact me, make a veiled threat, then go radio silent? Why hasn't she asked for money?"

Justin

Life is a precarious balancing act. Keep the plates spinning on each stick. Look away for a minute and lose one. Two of my spinning plates—Kay and Flash—were in danger. I would do anything to keep them. Even take the dangerous step of bringing another person into my situation.

"I knew it! I knew you'd pranked Lala into marrying you. How else could you have gotten her? But this is *seriously* whacked." Dex twisted the cap off his beer. "And epic. Pranking a woman into fake matrimony. You should write a book. There's a world of geeks out there who would pay for your secret."

I'd just come clean with Dex about my marriage-of-thwarting-the-ID-thief. "I didn't *prank* her into anything. I played on her sympathies. Now I'm paying her for her help. I hired her for a year to be my wife."

Dex raised one eyebrow and busted out laughing. "A thankless job, for sure! My cousin, the wife for hire. Shit." He paused. "Have you done her like I advised?"

I couldn't help myself. I grinned.

Dex gave me a thumbs-up. "Don't give me any details. She *is* my cousin. And like a sister to me." He cursed beneath his breath. "The moms are going to be so pissed with you when the divorce goes through."

I looked him in the eye. "Who says there's going to be a divorce?" I laughed. "Repeat that to Kay and I'll deny it."

"That's my man." Dex took a drink of beer and spun it to read the label. "Nice. I'll have to get me some of these." He grinned. "Or are they out of my price range?"

I shook my head at him. "Yeah, sure. It's billionaire-only beer."

He laughed. "So does this mean we're cousin-in-laws or not?"

I shrugged. "The hell if I know. It's a legal gray area."

"Oh, buddy. This is just too rich." He shook his head again. "That's a pun at your expense."

"If you have to explain a pun, it's not funny," I said.

We were drinking at my place, sitting in my office in front of the computer screen and the picture of the ID thief from Sunshine Sheri's show. Kay was out shopping and celebrating with Britt, who would be starting with Flash in two weeks. I'd wanted Kay out of the house while I talked with Dex.

"Clearly, you have a plan for winning Lala's love? And continuing this kind of, sort of marriage until death do you part." Dex was sprawled in my leather guest chair, legs spread wide. "If you find your perp, aren't you fast-tracking it to divorce court?"

I shook my head. "The postnup is ironclad. One year or no payout. Unless I change *my* mind."

"When hell freezes over, right?"

"You got that right." I took a long pull of beer and tapped the computer screen. "I have other reasons for delaying things."

"You mean the 30-60-90 windows for storing surveillance video until they overwrite?"

That was the thing about talking to Dex—he caught on quickly. I never needed to explain things to him. I nodded. "If the wedding chapel has pictures of the wedding on their security feeds..."

I felt the anger burbling up and took a deep breath to calm down. "I'm stalling. It's only been fifteen days. I need at least fifteen more. Then I'm going to bury her."

"I don't suppose you noticed the cameras? Things like were there any, were they obviously working, how ancient were they, that kind of thing?" Dex gave me a look that wasn't hopeful.

"My man in Reno has investigated. The wedding chapel has cameras in the lobby, none in the actual chapel. All the cameras are old-school videotape that's overwritten on a thirty-day cycle. We can't hack them. Believe me, I've fantasized about it."

Dex frowned. "Too damn bad. You must have been totally shitfaced to confuse that chick for Lala. My cousin is hot. This girl"—he pointed at my computer—"eh."

"Yeah." I still hadn't remembered more than snatches from that night. "What can I say? Alcohol goggles." I stared at the screen with him. "You've seen *The Hangover*. All the crazy shit that can happen when you're drunk and high. How you can completely forget it all. I'm convinced she drugged me."

Dex grunted. "*The Hangover* is a comedy."

"So is this—a black comedy."

Dex grinned. "It's a good thing I'm an old softie. And you're better than any guy Lala would pick on her own. I don't half mind being related to you by fake marriage and prankery. In the interests of my family, and my personal code of ethics and friendship, I'm honor-bound to help you."

He laughed. "This is going to be fun. First things first"—he pointed at my screen—"that picture is a piece of crap as far as using our software. We might be able to make do. If we have to. You've approached the guy who shot that? He could have more. Better shots. You'll have to pay, of course."

"I have another picture. A better picture," I said. "Kay doesn't know about it. This is just between us. Between the two shots, our software will have a better chance of finding her." I brought up the second picture.

Dex whistled softly, impressed.

"I've been running the second picture for about a week. No hits. The woman's good." I leaned back in my desk chair and downed a good portion of my beer, reveling in the relaxing buzz. I'd been too stressed lately. "What I didn't bring up is that there's a huge risk that the photographer's in on this scam, too. That I was set up. This is the ID thief's way of extorting more cash and skirting the law, staying anonymous and just inside the bounds. Presumably, if she's the one who directed the sale of this picture, it's a subtle threat without a paper trail. She's expecting me to pay big for the rest."

"That would be cunning of her." Dex casually leaned forward and studied her pictures onscreen. "That would be exceptionally cunning of her. I could almost admire her guts and style."

I nodded. "If it weren't being used to con me. The thing is, she can't have known who I was from the beginning or she would have married me under her real name. She, and her partner, if she has one, are working on the fly now. They'll screw up somewhere, if they haven't already."

"Are you going to bite and make an offer on some photos?" Dex's gaze was intelligent and piercing. He obviously had an opinion. This was like a test.

"I can't in under any circumstance, ever, admit I didn't marry the real Kayla. The whole house of cards falls apart if I do. I can't even hint at it."

Dex leaned forward. "So the answer is no?"

I didn't bother answering. It was a rhetorical question.

"If you're right, and she's behind it, you're taking a chance she'll escalate," Dex said.

"If she had something concrete, she would have come straight at me with it." I finished my beer, craving another.

"You could send a representative. Someone you trust who could front a plausible story." He raised an eyebrow and pointed at himself. "I could go as myself, Lala's cousin and your friend. I would claim she's embarrassed by them and furious and wants them out of circulation. That she's willing to pay."

I shook my head. "You obviously haven't been under the media's microscope. If it gets out Kay or I am willing to pay for such benign pictures, we'll have targets on our back. There will be photographers jumping out at us from everywhere."

Dex nodded, deep in thought. "You're right. You're taking a calculated risk. The problem for blackmailers is simple—if they make good on their threats and release what they have on you, they've lost their cash cow."

I nodded.

"What are you going to do?" Dex said.

"We have to find her and stop her. And stall as long as we can. Fifteen more days and she won't be able to prove she was the one I married. Sixty to ninety and she won't have any hotel video to use against me. As in, billionaire breaking vows on wedding night."

Dex shook his head. "When you fuck up, you really fuck up." He sounded impressed.

I shot him a dark look. "Got any good ideas?"

Dex pursed his lips and broke into a grin. "A few."

CHAPTER FIVE

Kayla

When we "got married," Jus had promised that he travelled most of the time. I would hardly feel married because he would be gone so often. I didn't know if he'd stayed in town on purpose the first two weeks of our married life. Or whether life and circumstances just lined up that way. But he made good on his promise the Monday after I had lunch with Britt celebrating her job offer from Flash. On Sunday afternoon, he announced he was flying out early the next morning on business to a bunch of locations. He'd arranged for Ophie to email me his itinerary and update me with any changes. Which were likely. Business meetings were rearranged, cancelled, or postponed all the time. Especially among the powerful.

Great. Just what I needed. Ophie more in the know about what Jus was up to than I was. Knowledge was power. And in this case, I *really* hated relinquishing it. To Ophie, of all people. Unfortunately, I couldn't see any way around it. Ophie had been perfectly pleasant to me. But I didn't trust her as a matter of the basic principles of love, war, and marriage. It wasn't rocket science—never trust a woman who wants your husband.

"I'll be back for the Fourth of July." Jus zipped his suitcase closed and looked around for his phone charger, distracted by packing.

"You'd better be. It's nearly two weeks away!" I watched him throw more chargers and accessories in his leather computer bag. "And a Friday night. I need a date."

Jus grinned at me, pleased by my outburst. "I'll hurry back as soon as I can."

I should have been relieved he was going. I needed time to think and sort out my feelings. When Jus was around things were complicated, to say the least. My heart didn't know what it was doing. And couldn't make up its mind about how it felt about him. Crazy, but I was already missing him. And he wasn't even gone yet.

I had a sudden inspiration. "We should throw a party for the Fourth here at the penthouse!"

My friends would love it. It would give me a chance to show off and really sell this marriage to them again. Happy domestic life as the billionaire's wife! Wasn't that sweet?

When again would I have a 360 view of the firework displays across the entire region—Seattle, Issaquah, south to Renton, and beyond. Not to mention we weren't more than a thousand yards or so away from the Bellevue show. More than half the time, it rained in Seattle on the Fourth. We joked that summer never started around here until July fifth. Having a warm, comfortable place and plenty of expensive booze was an added bonus enticement.

Jus shook his head. "Riggins always hosts a Fourth of July bash on his yacht. We boat around the sound all afternoon, eating and drinking. Then we park and watch the fireworks over Elliott Bay. With more eating and drinking. Attendance is mandatory. I've already accepted his invitation."

Did my face fall? It must have.

Jus pulled me into a hug. "Maybe next year we can coordinate with Riggins."

"Next year we'll be divorced." The words popped out of my mouth before I thought about them. They sounded harsh and hard-edged. And almost petulant.

Jus cleared his throat and looked away, embarrassed. "Yeah."

I sighed. As far as holidays, it was one and done around here. I had to make every holiday fabulous and full of memories before I left. Make the most out of this billionaire lifestyle. Although getting used to it probably wasn't the best idea.

Jus took the car service to the airport the next day. I got up and saw him off at the door with a kiss that was more than perfunctory on my part.

And I was on my own for two solitary weeks. So I thought. As it turned out, I had no time to grow bored. My days were completely booked. Compliments of my savvy personal assistant, Andrea. Meetings with the hospital's charitable board. Meetings at Flash with the buyers, arranging and organizing the samples that would be available for sale. Coordinating volunteer sign-ups for the sale. Meetings with donors and caterers. Florists. Friends. Shopping.

Magda and I grew closer. Maybe it wasn't good to get too friendly with the help. But I couldn't resist. When I got her going, she talked about Jus, always glowing about what a considerate employer he was. How he'd given her a large bonus when she needed help with her daughter's medical bills after a motorcycle accident. Really, did Jus have any faults?

More and more I felt like I was in a modern retelling of *Pride and Prejudice.* Where Lizzie finds out the true, caring character of Mr. Darcy. Why, he wasn't proud at all! Only in my case it was more like *Geek and Great Guy.* Everywhere I turned, people loved and admired Jus.

The part-time maid came and went, tidying up after me. But she rarely spoke. I never got to know her.

Even through all the busyness, I missed Jus. And so did poor little Data. She moped around and looked expectantly toward the door every time someone came or went.

On Monday night, I replaced Jus in bed with his pillow, curling up next to it as I lay awake in bed. How could I have gotten so used to his presence in just a few weeks? Outside my door, Data whimpered and cried, refusing to sleep. I relented and took her into bed with me, letting her sleep curled at the foot of the bed. It was a dangerous precedent to set, but without it, neither of us was going to get any sleep.

Concerned, the next day I asked Magda about it. "What does Jus usually do with Data when he's gone? Is he aware she cries all night?"

"Mr. Justin hasn't had Data long," she told me. "When he's gone at night, I take her home with me."

So there it was. Mystery solved. I was relieved. I didn't like the thought of Data all alone and crying, during the day or during the night. And so I indulged myself in carrying out the threat I'd made when I first met Data—I bought a dog purse. Because, yes, rich people must carry their dogs around in purses or they break the stereotype. And besides, it was a simple kind of evil fun to imagine Justin's response when he got home.

I mentioned, partly in jest, the struggles of trying to find a doggy purse that coordinated with my outfits to Marla on one of my visits to Flash.

"A doggy and me event!" Marla gave me a thumbs-up. "That's brilliant! We'll see what we can do."

Two days later, Marla called and asked me to bring Data in for photo shoot for one of Flash's upcoming events featuring fashion accessories for pets. For my trouble, I walked away with several rhinestone collars and leashes for Data. Jus was so going to kill me over the chickification of his dog.

Justin's schedule was so crazy that we rarely had time to talk, and our texts were infrequent. When we did talk, he was all in. The excited sound of his voice on the phone made me smile. "How's Data? Does she miss me?"

"She's fine!" I resisted a snigger. I wanted him to be totally surprised when he got home. "We're getting along great."

"Oh, no. What have you done to my dog?" He sounded way too suspicious. "You haven't put her in a purse. Kay, tell me you haven't put her in a purse!"

I laughed and sidestepped the question. "I've decided to take you up on your offer and add a few personal touches to the penthouse and closet. What's my budget?"

It was weird. But with Jus away, I suddenly had the urge to leave my fingerprints on his life. Call it vanity. Call it wanting to sell the marriage—anyone who knew me would expect me to make changes to Justin's place. You could even call it optimism.

Jus preloaded a credit card for my use. It must be said, as shallow as it sounds, that using that card was thrilling. As I spent, I wondered if Jus would like what I was buying.

I visited Sophia and Vicki. In an attempt to win their favor after stealing Jus away, I brought them matching mother-daughter sundresses and headbands. And asked them to be models in the fashion show I was planning as part of the sample sale. It was my idea to dress up models in outfits comprised of samples as inspiration for the shoppers. And have buyers on hand to help shoppers if they needed help. I even showed them a picture of Data in her carrying purse.

"I want a doggy like that one," Sophia told Vicki. "So I can carry it around in my purse."

The next time I went to see her, I brought her a toy stuffed Pomsky in a purse.

Everywhere I went, it seemed, even the hospital, I bumped into Lazer. It was like a huge cosmic joke—*See what you could have had, Kayla. If only you hadn't jumped at ten million.* Fate seemed to be shoving us in each other's faces. And laughing at us.

About the tenth time it happened—in the pet store, of all places; I was buying special new doggy treats for Data, Lazer needed more fish food and a new filter for his aquarium—he said, "I must be unintentionally stalking you."

"Unintentionally?"

"Subliminally? Is that a thing?" The sexy look in his eyes would stop the hardest heart.

"Maybe I'm subliminally stalking *you*?" I couldn't keep the flirt out of my voice and body language.

He laughed. "I'd like to think so." He was so smooth. "We meet too often for mere coincidence."

Lazer was fun to flirt with. Hot to look at. Charming. And out of my reach. We got along so well it was scary. I couldn't get past the feeling that on another lifeline, in an alternate universe, he and I could have been extremely happy together. If only there hadn't been a Jus. But no Jus, no way I would have met Lazer. It was a Catch-22 situation of the highest order. Every time I got myself together and got close to getting myself out of the warring emotions I was in, fate upped the number of bombing runs. And threw me into confusion again by throwing me in Lazer's path.

When Jus left on the twenty-sixth, Seattle was its normal, pleasant, slightly cool, sometimes summery, showery self. On the twenty-seventh, the jet stream changed course, and Seattle began to bake. Record heat stretched day after day as the mercury climbed. Buns became the most popular women's hairstyle in the city. And Costco couldn't keep fans or air conditioners in stock.

The thing people have to understand about Seattle is that it is tied with San Francisco as the least air-conditioned city in the country. Fewer than one in ten people have air conditioning. I had it in the penthouse, of course. But my old apartment? Nope. I would have been sweltering.

Usually Seattle's onshore flow cools it off at night. A persistent high-pressure center had spun our onshore flow out to sea. Tensions flared. And while Seattle baked, I was fiddling like Nero. Enjoying the high life. Enjoying running into Lazer. Or maybe I was simply playing with fire.

After one of my many meetings at Flash, I was supposed to meet Britt downtown for dinner. I'd already arrived at the restaurant when I got Britt's message that she had to cancel. Something about a problem with the paperwork she had to fill out before she could start at Flash. She was running over there to take care of it. But she didn't want to hold me up. Let's reschedule!

I was hungry. I decided to dine alone. Coincidentally, I ran into Lazer again. He was also dining alone. His business client had cancelled on him. Lazer invited me to join him while we laughed about this seeming like another setup. Another us-subliminally-stalking-each-other incident.

Maybe I shouldn't have joined him out in public when Jus was gone. But it seemed rude not to. It was purely innocent, anyway. What could possibly happen in public? We laughed too easily. Drank too much. Put our heads together too closely. And stared too long into each other's eyes.

When I got home, I felt guilty. And lonely. Lazer was fun. But I longed for Jus and his eagerness. And the way he made me laugh.

July second, the day before Jus was due home, I was eager and excited for his return. Magda and I had planned a special meal for him. I'd bought a pair of pasties and a hot little thong number to surprise him with. I wondered, delighted with myself, if he'd fare any better removing the pasties than he had with the chicken cutlets. They wouldn't stick to the mirror, that was for sure. But was there anything more than sex between us? Despite the occasional fun of flirting with Lazer, my feelings for Jus were growing.

But I was a broken vessel. Unwilling to slap my heart out there to be stomped on first again. My disastrous relationship with Eric had really done a number on me. And I still wondered if Jus was my rebound guy. Or were the beginnings of love I was feeling real?

Sometimes I longed for that old crush Jus had had on me in college. But crushes weren't real love. And real love was what I wanted next time around.

Magda had already gone home when I got a text from Lazer. He was in my lobby. This seemed to be a case of intentional stalking. I buzzed him up.

"You must be in a panic," he said as soon as he walked in. He looked so serious I almost laughed.

"Must I?" I frowned and smiled at the same time, totally confused. "Why?"

He pulled a sparkling tennis bracelet out of his pocket. "I was at Flash meeting with Riggins. They said you lost this. I had to bring it right over. I couldn't trust it with anyone else."

The bracelet dangling from his fingers looked very similar to the diamond tennis bracelet Jus had given me. But why did he think it was mine? I held up my wrist for him to see. "That's sweet of you, but I have mine. See?"

He frowned. "Then whose is this?"

I laughed and took it from him, inspecting it. "Hmmm...I don't know. But it's gold plate at best. And I'm guessing these are crystals, not real diamonds. Still, a nice bracelet. Though not hideously expensive. It looks like a sample of something Flash would sell." I grabbed his hand, turned it palm up, and pressed the bracelet back into it.

Our eyes locked. I felt a spark. I was sure he did, too.

"I'll take it back to Flash." He dropped it in his pocket.

"I was just sitting out on the deck, enjoying the evening view. Care to join me?" I probably shouldn't have asked.

"I can stay for a minute or two." He smiled graciously.

"I was thinking of making myself a drink. Can I get you something?" Offering a drink was definitely a no-no. But after the busy day I'd had, I needed something to relax me. And it seemed only polite.

"A beer's fine. Jus always has some good ones around."

"Lager? Ale? Pale? Dark?"

"A dark ale sounds great."

I got him one from the fridge. When I handed it and a glass to him, our fingers brushed. I felt another spark. So did he. I saw it in his eyes. We sat out on the sofa on the balcony, side by side, drinking and looking out at Bellevue and Seattle beyond.

"This heat." Lazer opened the first few buttons of his shirt and rolled up his sleeves.

He'd come straight from work. He was still dressed for business in his tailored, expensive clothes. I was in shorts and a tank top and flip-flops.

Our arms brushed. Our thighs touched as we talked about nothing. He drank his beer. I drank my mixed drink. It was so easy to flirt with a man like Lazer, who was skilled at flirting back. It meant nothing to either of us. It really didn't. We weren't in public. No one was around, so what was the harm?

Our fingers brushed again. Our eyes met. I smiled at him. His arm was over the back of the outdoor sofa in a position that could almost be construed as around me.

I lifted the hair off my neck.

"Hot?"

I rolled my eyes. "When will this heat wave end?" I may have been talking about us. "A few more days and we'll have the record."

His fingers slid down the sofa back and lightly skimmed my neck, raising goosebumps at his touch. My breath caught. Our gazes locked. I released my hair, letting it tumble over my shoulders, down my back, over Lazer's fingers that were still at the nape of my neck. Suddenly, he cupped the back of my head and pulled me toward him.

I closed my eyes. Our lips met. His were warm and insistent. Skilled. Expert at extracting sighs from women. He smelled like expensive cologne. And tasted like Justin's expensive beer—

At the thought of Jus, I came to my senses and started pulling away at the same time he let me go. I wasn't acting my part. And part of me wasn't acting at all.

We spoke at once. "I'm sorry." "I shouldn't have. What was I thinking?"

We laughed awkwardly, embarrassed.

"It's my fault," he said, acting the gentleman. "All that subliminal stalking." His jaw set. "Since I met you I've been wondering what it would be like to kiss you." He stared at me. "Lucky Justin."

"No, it's my fault. Sometimes I barely feel like a married woman. I haven't learned how to turn the flirt off yet."

"Not flirting and acting married is an acquired skill, I'm sure." He set his beer bottle on the table in front of us. "I should go."

I nodded and walked him to the door.

He cupped my chin and tipped my face up. "If only we'd met sooner."

I stared at him until he dropped his hand. "This stays between us." I held his gaze. "I don't want to hurt Jus."

Not that he necessarily would be hurt by me kissing another guy, given what a fake our marriage was. But I'd promised not to embarrass him. Or give us away. And this probably qualified. Worse, there was a big part of me that felt like I had betrayed him. I had no idea where that feeling came from.

Lazer nodded. "Of course."

I watched Lazer walk away, wondering what I'd just done. And how it must look to him. I hoped he kept his word.

CHAPTER SIX

Justin

I was scheduled to fly home late on the third. My meetings got pushed out. I flew home on the fourth. My flight was late. I was supposed to arrive at one, in plenty of time for Riggins' scheduled three o'clock departure. I didn't get home until three thirty. I texted Kay from the plane and told her to go ahead to the party. I didn't want her missing the boat. I would join up with them as soon as I could.

She texted back, *How? We'll be out in the middle of the sound.*

I responded, *Trust me.* And grinned. Some people could be so naïve. She still wasn't used to living the billionaire's life.

A speedboat and driver were waiting for me at the marina. I called Riggins for coordinates and put my driver in touch with his. It felt good to be out on the water. I was so damn eager to see Kay again.

A crowd gathered on the back of Riggins' boat as mine approached. I felt like James Bond on a mission as we sped toward it. Riggins should have slowed down the damn boat. But he had his driver gun it as we neared. It was just like Riggins to pull that stunt. There was nothing he enjoyed more than a chase.

I shouted to my driver over the roar of the engine, "Catch that yacht and step on it!"

I already had a beer in my hand. I leaned back, adjusted my sunglasses, and put my feet up on the side of the boat, enjoying the feel of the spray as we glided across the water. It was hotter than hell on land. But cool and pleasant on the water. If Riggins thought he could outrun us in his state-of-the-art yacht, he was full of bat shit.

Riggins leaned against the back rail, waving me, or some would say egging me, on. Pointing. Exaggerated shrugging. Glancing at his watch. Tapping it. Miming, *Come on, buddy. What are you waiting for? Catch up and join us.*

Riggins' yacht was a real white beauty. He could comfortably sleep eight to ten people in his four staterooms. The body was sleek, curved, and modern. The back deck covered except for the sunbathing porch. Lazer, with his arm around a bikini-clad girl, joined Riggins on the lower back deck, laughing while I gained on them.

Kay had been lounging and sunning on a lounge chair on the main deck. She stood now, too, joining the crowd. She wore a skimpy red, white, and blue bikini tied together at her breasts with a red bow. I didn't have much fashion sense, but I thought the top was retro. High-heeled navy flip-flop-style sandals studded with red beads and rhinestones gave her several inches and made her legs look like they belonged on a runway. Her long blond hair blew in the breeze. She looked just as hot and gorgeous as she had on the beach at college. When I had to eye her from afar. Wait a minute! Wasn't I watching her from a distance now and still chasing her?

I smiled to myself. Different circumstances altogether. I was racing toward my wife. I'd fantasized about a moment like this for years.

She brushed her hair out of her face, waving vigorously to me with one arm. Was that my dog she had in the other? At the sight of Kay, my heart did a furiously happy cartwheel.

I fought to keep my cool exterior, leaning back and taking a swig of beer as we closed the gap and Riggins surrendered. He finally slowed the boat enough so we could pull up to the swimming deck and came down from the middle deck to greet me.

"Permission to come aboard, captain!" I saluted him.

"You mean I can deny you?" Riggins grinned and saluted back.

"Not really. I'll just stage a hostile takeover of your vessel." I stood as my driver kept us even with the yacht.

Riggins offered me a hand over. "Nice of you to finally join us."

I set my beer down, ignored the hand he offered, and swung over from my boat to his. "Nice of you to make it so easy."

He laughed. "Get yourself something fresh to drink."

Data still in her arms, Kay rushed down the steps from the deck above toward me. She looked so damn hot and lovely she made my heart ache. I swelled with pride. We were in public. I could let my true feelings show.

"Jus!" She kissed me as if she'd missed me, maybe a little too enthusiastically, while Data barked excitedly.

Who was Kay trying to impress?

"I've missed you so much!" Her eyes sparkled.

Maybe her words were true, maybe not. In any case, they made me happier than they should have.

I scratched Data behind the ears. She was wearing a red, white, and blue collar that exactly matched the straps of Kay's shoes, and a doggy headband. "What have you done to my dog?"

Data barked again, wagging her tail as she answered for Kay.

Kay shrugged. "Dressed her for the Fourth." Her tone was way too innocent.

"I told you not to girl up my dog." I took Data from her as we climbed the stairs together to the middle deck. When we reached the deck, I took the headband off Data. And caught a glimpse of a red, white, and blue bag sitting beside the chair Kay had been in.

"Have you been putting my dog in a purse? Damn it, Kay."

She took Data back from me and set her on the deck. Then she wrapped her arms around me and kissed me. It was hard to stay mad when she was nearly naked in my arms.

Riggins tapped me on the shoulder. "If you want a room, help yourself." He laughed.

I was tempted. The bedrooms on Riggins' boat were large, private, and luxurious.

Everything on the boat was elegant and modern, with clean lines and square cuts. Tan sofas, white pillows, and beech-colored tongue-in-groove wooden floors. Chrome fixtures. Chrome-edged glass tables.

We sailed farther out into Elliott Bay. It was crowded on the sound. Loud. Hot. The hottest Fourth on record, the weather report said. But it was nice on the water and Riggins had air conditioning inside the ship.

Kay threw on a sexy white cover-up dress for the sit-down salmon dinner prepared by Riggins' personal chef. Riggins' white and stainless steel dining room was my favorite part of his boat. Dark wood tables edged in stainless steel. White chairs. Black lamps. Hard lines. I ate too much. Drank too much. Looked at Kay too much.

Riggins went on again about buying a submarine. Every once in a while he got it in his head that it would be great fun to cruise around the bottom of the sound in a submarine. If he started talking about it, you couldn't shut him up.

"Do they make personal submarines?" Kay asked.

Oh crap. She and Lazer's new girl were the two people at the table who didn't know better than to walk into his trap. And he'd suckered Kay in. He launched into a soliloquy about submarine specs. While she leaned forward and listened intently.

Kay was animated and happy. Bubbly. Charming to everyone throughout the evening. My friends all loved her. Some a little too much. Yes, I knew I was wading in dangerous territory. If I lost Kay, would they take her side?

There was something going on between her and Lazer. They were awkward with each other in a way they never had been before. Shit, they'd hit it off from the start. Now they avoided each other, though they tried not to be obvious about it. Were almost distant. They tried too hard to be pleasant to each other. It was only a veneer. What the hell had happened? Whatever it was, it was good for me.

I smiled to myself. *If Kay isn't interested in Lazer anymore, it opens the door for me.*

Kay leaned against the front rail on the top deck as we watched the fireworks. I stood behind her with my arms around her, wanting her badly. I was horny as hell. And happy. Happy to be home. Happy to have Kay waiting for me. Happy with the progress I'd made. Thirty days were nearly up. We were nearly that much safer.

Kayla

By the time we got home, we were both drunk. Justin wanted sex. That much was clear from the time he first nuzzled me on the yacht. I was happy to have him home. And feeling so guilty I would have done anything to make it up to him.

Inside the penthouse, we settled Data into her bed. She was exhausted and nervous. The fireworks had upset her. She'd spent the night cowering in either my arms or Justin's. I was glad I hadn't left her alone in the penthouse. The booms would have scared her even through our fairly soundproofed walls.

I wrapped my arms around Jus and ran my fingers over his beard. "Did you miss me?"

"Tragically."

"That much?" I brushed his lips with a light kiss. "Did you fantasize about me?"

"You are my fantasy, Kay." His voice was husky.

"Good answer." I looked into his eyes, feeling buzzed and flirty and ready for sex. Being buzzed was dangerous business. "If I could fulfill one of your fantasies, what would it be?"

His Adam's apple bobbed, but he didn't hesitate. "Let me make love to you up against the glass wall of our bedroom. While you're wearing the heels you have on now and nothing else. From behind while you face out to the city."

The thought of making love against the windows excited me.

"That's an advanced maneuver." I held his gaze. "Are you up for it?"

His eyes became round and dark. "One way to find out."

"Then what are we waiting for?" I pulled him by the hand to the dark bedroom and shut the door, keeping Data out.

He stood silhouetted against the lights of the city in the windows. I pulled my cover-up off over my head. He kicked off his shoes and shed his shirt. I untied my bikini top and let it drop. He slid out of his shorts and briefs. I stood in my bikini bottom and Fourth of July heels, facing him.

"Take off your swimsuit bottoms." His voice was low and sexy, filled with desire that took my breath away.

"Why? They won't get in the way. Much." I was staring at him, boldly, challenging him to take control. His face was in shadow, unreadable in the dark.

"Take them off." He turned just enough for me to see he was erect and ready.

I was supposed to be the one tantalizing him. But it was the other way around. I was totally tight and hot for him. I looked him in the eye in the darkness, with the lights of the city sparkling behind him in the window, and took a step toward him. I stumbled, laughing drunkenly. "What are you going to do about it?"

Jus leaped forward and caught me, swept me into his arms, and carried me to the window, kissing me on the way with a hot trail of kisses down my throat. He set me down, hooked a finger in the string of my bikini bottom, and tugged it down in a Houdini-like move. I stepped out of it and kicked it away.

"I missed you." He cupped my breast and took me in a kiss so deep and passionate, it took my breath away. "Every minute I was away."

It wasn't exactly a declaration of love. "You mean you missed sex." I grabbed his dick and stroked it.

He caught my chin in his hand and stared into my eyes. "No, I mean I missed *you*."

Something about the way he said it went straight to my heart. I let go of him and stared back. If his eyes were the windows to his soul, they were dark and unreadable now.

He released my chin, took me by the waist, and spun me around to face the windows. "I want you to *see* fireworks while we make some."

"That's a nice visual. You're so corny and sweet, baby." As I stared out over the landscape and felt his heat behind me, a round of red and green sparkles burst from over the hills near the water. "You should write greeting cards."

He laughed and whispered in my ear. "When? In my spare time? I use every minute of that thinking of you."

Oh, damn, Jus, I thought. *You tease and dance all around it, but you don't say you love me. Do you think it's too soon? Or has it been way too long? Will you wait until the day before our divorce before you decide? Will I? Will either of us ever admit to what's growing between us?*

I didn't say anything back that gave him any indication of how I felt. That I was falling for him. I refused to make a mistake. A mistake could cost me everything. He had all the power in this relationship. He needed to say it first.

He pressed up behind me, sliding between my legs as he kissed my neck. "Bend over."

"Any way you want it." I spread my legs into a wide stance and obeyed, bracing my hands against the cool, thick glass.

"Farther." His voice was husky with lust.

I complied, putting both my forearms and palms against the window now. What would Magda think of palm prints on the windows?

Jus bent over me, kissing my back, tickling me softly with his beard as his kisses trailed up my spine. He slid a finger between my legs. Then deep inside me. I gasped as he thrust with his finger and found a spot that made me weak in the knees.

"There it is," he mumbled, sounding amazed and pleased with himself as he pulled his finger out.

He wrapped one arm around my waist and slid in from behind. His first thrust pushed my breasts against the glass between my arms. I gasped. What would Magda think of breast prints on the glass?

His next thrust pushed all rational, and irrational, thought from my mind. I gasped. He had, indeed, found the spot. I'd begun to think my G-spot was imaginary. As the cities sparkled in front of me, and fireworks burst forth in irregular intervals, Jus pushed me against the glass time and time again, holding me tightly around the waist.

The main fireworks shows were long over. But our private fireworks were just revving up. I arched my back, helping him hit the spot. I'd never felt so full of a man before. So breathless and weak with need and desire. So on the edge for so long.

The moon was large and round, nearly full, brilliantly bright. The man in the moon clear, almost a voyeur as he looked down on us. Lights were on in condos and offices below us. I should have been shy. But no one could see us. Thank goodness, because my face would have given me away.

Jus pounded into me again. I gasped. For some reason, I focused on the near image in the glass, rather than the distant scenery. I was startled to see my reflection. *Oh, crap.* Jus was mirrored in the glass, too, watching me, watching us with an intense, searching look as he drove deep inside me. What had he seen? What had I shown him? Why was he holding back?

"Finish it, Jus. Just *finish* it." I'd never begged a guy before.

He tightened his grip around my waist, holding me firmly against him, and drove it home. The pleasure was so intense, I screamed, a high, throaty cry of pure pleasure. And maybe his name. There was no conscious thought attached to it.

A spectacular round of fireworks burst over the near hill. *Damn you, Jus, and your fireworks talk. Damn you for being right.*

I had never been a screamer, always thought it was put on and faked when I heard other girls. Now I knew.

Jus caught my startled expression in our reflection in the window. As my legs went weak, he grunted, called out my name—at least I think it was my name—and collapsed against me, his chest pressed to my back. His bearded cheek soft against my shoulders. He held me tight, he held me up as my legs trembled, as we caught our breath.

"I can barely stand," I said when I could finally find breath enough.

He laughed softly. "Don't worry. I got you." He turned his head, kissed the top of my spine, and ran his tongue along it until I shivered while he held me up.

"Are you trying to kill me?" I stared at him in the glass.

He gave me an odd expression. "Yeah, that's exactly my plan. Kill you with my lovemaking." He slipped out of me, resting his chin on my back while I hung my head and took a deep breath.

"I'm not kidding, Jus. Really, my legs are shaky."

He spun me around into his arms and carried me to the bed. "That good, huh?"

"Oh, shut up. Yes, you get an A this time."

His answering grin was sweet and adorable, sexy in a way I hadn't thought possible. It made my heart ache. "Not just for effort?"

"Oh, Jus, that was for way more than effort. That was an A for *every*thing. Now put me down."

He pulled back the covers with one hand and set me down in the middle of a pile of pillows. He climbed into bed and lay next to me with his head in his hand. "I thought you weren't a screamer?"

"Don't get cocky, kid." I brushed his nose with the tip of my finger.

"Too late." He grabbed my hand and moved it to his hard dick.

Just then Data barked and whined to be let in.

Jus frowned. "Settle down and go back to bed, Data."

I bit my lip. "I hate to tell you this, but that's what she's trying to do."

The furrows in his forehead deepened. "You didn't?"

I shrugged. "You were gone and we were both lonely. She's used to sleeping with me now. And probably scared by the fireworks still going off."

He grumbled and got up to let the dog in.

"Get me a nightgown while you're up!"

He gave me a dark look as Data bounded in and I scooped her up. He watched while she settled herself in at the foot of the bed between us and gave us a satisfied look.

"Nightgown?"

He froze.

I laughed. "I'm not traumatizing her further by doing anything X-rated in front of her. She's just a baby."

He cursed beneath his breath and grabbed me a nightie.

I woke up in the morning with a pounding hangover. I plodded into the bathroom and ran myself a glass of water to take a painkiller. My birth control pills were right there, too. I might as well take the two pills together. I popped the pill out of its pill pack. As I tossed the two pills into my mouth, I thought I heard something drop, something small. I swallowed my glass of water and looked around. I didn't see anything. My head was too thick to think.

I went back to bed to sleep the rest of the hangover off. Jus was up, talking on the phone.

He hung up and gave me a sheepish look. "That was Riggins. We have an emergency on our hands. I have to fly out ASAP. I'm meeting him at the airport."

"On the Fourth of July weekend?" I didn't want him to go.

"Fourth of July doesn't mean shit in the rest of the world." He came over and took me in his arms. "I'm sorry. It's not my first choice."

I touched his arm. "How long will you be gone?"

He sighed. "Weeks, at least. I was supposed to leave again on Wednesday for a week-and-a-half trip. Now there's no point in coming home in between."

"No," I said. But I didn't mean it. I had no right to complain. I was only his wife-for-hire.

"Look on the bright side," he said. "The less we're together, the less chance we have of screwing up and giving ourselves away." He sounded almost rueful.

Oh, boy. He had no idea how much I could screw up while he was gone. "The gossip rags will say you've tired of me already," I said with a tease in my voice.

He should have laughed. Instead his expression became serious. "They would be wrong."

He rushed off without noticing, or at least commenting on, the changes I was making to the penthouse. And left me with a warning: "Keep my dog out of your purse."

CHAPTER SEVEN

Kayla

I was late. Late. Late. Late. *Late.*

Say a word often enough and it starts to sound ridiculous. Even the idea of being late was absurd. One of those inconveniences of the body.

But it happened from time to time. Even though I was on the pill. It was a wakeup call. Life's way of warning me to be more careful. In college, I'd had two pregnancy scares. Who hadn't had at least one? Eric was a douche about them both times, yelling at me to be more careful. As if birth control was my sole responsibility. I was taking the pill. What more did he want? He was the one who didn't like condoms.

I wasn't particularly happy about being late. But I wasn't worried. Or scared. I did wonder, though: if Jus had been around, would I have told him like I did Eric? Eric and I had at least been a real couple. Which meant we dealt with stuff together, even if we fought about it.

It was probably just stress. Stress did crazy things to my body. I'd been so busy, busy, busy while Jus was gone. Going, going, going, wrapped up in my Justin's-away lifestyle while July rapidly slid toward August and our upcoming honeymoon. Trying not to think about missing him. Or how deep I was getting in our deception. Our how much I was in love with his dog and enjoyed living in his penthouse and spending his money. And how much I thought I was actually falling in love with him. And how I'd even resorted to buying the Sport Fresh scent of deodorant because it smelled guy-like and reminded me of Jus. Wearing the Sport Fresh scent was a cheap way for the man-less girl to pretend she had a guy around. I was pathetic.

The remedy for a late period was simple—take a pregnancy test and put my mind at ease. Before Jus got home. Then destroy the evidence.

He'd been gone for weeks, always promising to come back soon. He had to make good on it sometime.

If things had felt complicated in college, when I slunk down the row at the drugstore and bought a pregnancy test on the sly, things were way more complicated now. If the media got hold of me buying a pregnancy test, it would be all over the news. And I couldn't very well ask any of my friends to buy me one, either. This was top-secret business. So I ordered my usual brand online, from my old single girl's account so Jus wouldn't find out about it, and had it delivered same day. It seemed like a waste and a lot of stealth to go through for peace of mind. All this secrecy was getting to me.

When I went into the bathroom first thing the next morning to take the test, I still wasn't worried. I felt no test pressure at all. I had no symptoms. No tiredness. No sore breasts. Nothing. No reason to worry. And this brand was reliable and comforting. It hadn't let me down yet by giving me the two bars of pregnancy positive doom.

I thought about the last time Jus and I had been together. Great sex didn't make you pregnant. I mean, not any more than crappy sex could get you pregnant. There was no need to be superstitious.

I opened the test, took out the stick, stuck it in midstream, and set it on the counter to cure. My cell rang on the nightstand in the bedroom. Jus was calling. I rushed out of the bathroom and grabbed it, feeling guilty. Like I'd been caught in the middle of a nefarious act.

"Hey, Kay! How's my baby?"

My pulse raced at the sound of his voice. His question was badly timed. "You mean the dog?"

I hoped he meant the dog. On top of everything else, he couldn't possibly be psychic, too, and suspect I was in the middle of testing to see if he was going to be a daddy.

"Yeah, sure, the dog!" He laughed. "I couldn't possibly be calling *you* baby."

"We aren't in public. No one can hear us, so you don't need to keep up the act." I sat on the bed and glanced at the clock. Another few minutes and I would be in the clear.

"Mom called. Did she send you the itinerary she has planned for us in Naples?"

Hearing his voice was sweet, but I was barely listening. Too distracted. "Yeah. She did."

He started talking about Italy excitedly. Hinting at surprises while I watched the minutes tick by and got up to check on my test. I was only half listening as I wandered into the bathroom.

I picked up the stick just as Jus said, "How are things going on your end in Seattle? Kay? Kay, are you still there?"

Gina Robinson is the award-winning author of the contemporary new adult romances *Rushed, Crushed, Reckless Longing, Reckless Secrets,* and *Reckless Together* and the Agent Ex series of humorous romantic suspense novels. She's currently working on the next installment of Switched at Marriage.

Connect with Gina Online:

My Website: http://www.ginarobinson.com/
Twitter: @ginamrobinson
Facebook: www.facebook.com/GinaRobinsonAuthor

www.ingramcontent.com/pod-product-compliance
Lightning Source LLC
LaVergne TN
LVHW020645100826
845148LV00012B/2340

* 9 7 8 0 6 9 2 4 9 2 6 1 1 *